PRiNCESSES, iNC.

ALSO BY MARI MANCUSI

Golden Girl

PRINCESSES, INC.

MARI MANCUSI

ALADDIN M!X
New York London Toronto Sydney New Delhi

ALADDIN M!X

Simon & Schuster Children's Publishing Division
1230 Avenue of the Americas, New York, New York 10020
First Aladdin M!X paperback edition July 2017
Text copyright © 2017 by Marianne Mancusi
Cover illustration copyright © 2017 by Andrea Fernandez
Also available in an Aladdin hardcover edition.
For information about special discounts for bulk purchases, please contact Simon & Schuster Special Sales at 1-866-506-1949 or business@simonandschuster.com.
The Simon & Schuster Speakers Bureau can bring authors to your live event.
For more information or to book an event contact the Simon & Schuster Speakers Bureau at 1-866-248-3049 or visit our website at www.simonspeakers.com.
Cover designed by Jessica Handelman
Interior designed by Mike Rosamilia
The text of this book was set in Arno Pro.
Manufactured in the United States of America 0617 OFF
2 4 6 8 10 9 7 5 3 1
This book has been cataloged with the Library of Congress.
ISBN 978-1-4814-7901-1 (hc)
ISBN 978-1-4814-7900-4 (pbk)
ISBN 978-1-4814-7902-8 (eBook)

To my mother-in-law, Mary Ann, and my husband, Jacob, who help me make my own princess costumes come to life!

1

He turned . . . on a dime. His eyes locked onto Sarah—as if finally seeing her for the very first time. Her breath caught in her throat. Her heart pounded in her chest. He opened his mouth to speak.

"Sarah?"

"Y-yes . . . Collin?" she squeaked.

Was he going to tell her at last? How he really felt about her? Was it the same way she felt about him?

She knew only one thing for sure. His next words—whatever they were—would change her life . . . forever.

"And . . . to be continued."

"Wait, *what*?"

My best friend, Sarah, gaped at me with bug eyes as I set my three-ring binder down next to my lunch tray and grabbed a fork, stuffing a big bite of mashed potatoes into my mouth.

"What do you mean, 'to be continued,' Hailey?" she demanded. "You mean, like, to be continued after you swallow that obscenely large bite of food you just shoveled into your mouth?"

I hid a smile before swallowing. "No. I mean, like, that's all I've got so far."

"What? NO!" she practically shrieked, prompting a warning look from one of the cafeteria monitors. As the star of most of our school plays, Sarah had a reputation for being the loudest girl in the room, even when not onstage, where it was actually necessary.

She scowled and lowered her voice—barely—and leaned over the table, her green eyes locked on me. "How can that be all you have?" she hissed. "How could you just leave off there like . . . that? How could you just sit there now, like everything's all fine and cool, while your bestie's been reduced to a slobbering mess on the cafeteria floor?"

I shrugged. "It's called a cliff-hanger."

"It's *called* cruel and unusual punishment," she corrected with a moan, running her hands through her long red hair, tangling them in her curls. "In fact, I'm pretty sure there's some kind of Geneva Convention act outlawing this kind of thing—especially when done to one's best friend."

She grabbed the binder I'd been reading from, as if she still didn't believe there wasn't more somehow, hidden in the margins. Or printed with invisible ink, maybe. Her desperation made me grin.

"So, does this mean you like my story?" I asked, trying not to laugh.

She tossed the binder back at me. "I *hate* it," she declared. "I hate it with the fiery passion of a thousand burning suns!" She groaned loudly. "Seriously, Hailey—how can you just leave off like that? Right when Collin's going to tell me . . . well, whatever it is he's going to tell me. Which is clearly something awesome, obviously. It *is* going to be awesome, right? And romantic? Definitely something romantic!"

She gave me an expectant look. I shook my head slowly. She collapsed back onto her seat, staring up at the ceiling. "Did you know I hate you? 'Cause I really hate you."

I reached over to give her a comforting pat on the arm, knowing she would *really* hate me if she knew the truth—that I had a brand-new chapter back home on my computer, just waiting to be printed out. But I'd learned all too well that it was way more fun to dish them out in small portions . . . and keep her and my other friends in suspense.

It was funny: I'd always loved to write. Even when I was a little kid. Problem was, no one ever wanted to read what I wrote. (Except my dad, before he got too busy with work.) Then one day I got this idea to write Collin Prince fan fiction, with my three best friends—Sarah, Madison, and Kalani—as supporting characters. Now I practically had to fend my readership off with a stick. Which was more than a little awesome for any budding writer, and only encouraged me to torture them even more with each and every installment.

Collin Prince, for those of you who didn't know— (and seriously, you'd have to be living under a rock!)— was sixteen years old and the number one YouTube star in the country, with his videos averaging ten to fifteen million views . . . the *day* he put them online. He was not only super famous and super funny. He was also *super cute*. Like the cutest guy you've ever seen. We were, all four, in love with him—and had been ever since one rainy Saturday afternoon a year ago when we were stuck inside with nothing to do and followed this viral video train that led us to his page.

Since then we'd watched *all* his videos. Every single one. Even the kind of gross ones he made for his guy fans. ('Cause, let's face it—guys could be gross.) Like the one time he blended up an entire McDonald's Happy Meal and drank the whole thing from a *Star Wars* sippy cup— which was hilarious, but a little nauseating, to be honest. Still, we forgave him. 'Cause he was Collin Prince. And he was *so cute*.

We even made up a little unofficial fan club. And we had meetings every Saturday morning in Madison's bedroom. (She had the biggest bedroom of the four of us, and her parents were usually out playing golf.) We'd cuddle up on her giant king-size canopy bed and watch Collin's latest videos on her iPad without any adults peering over our shoulders and asking questions.

Adults never "got" Collin Prince. Which, in my

opinion, just proved the science of brain cells dying as you age. 'Cause, seriously? One look into his deep brown eyes and anyone who wasn't a goner clearly wasn't human, either.

I realized Sarah was still giving me a dirty look. "I'm sorry," I said, holding up my hands in innocence. "I wanted to write more—I really did. But I had to get to my homework. Those pre-algebra equations won't solve themselves, you know."

Truth be told, I had actually spent more time video-gaming last night than math-homeworking. But she didn't need to know that, seeing as I didn't have a death wish. Instead I gave her a pitying smile. "Guess you'll just have to find some other way to cling to life until tomorrow."

"Oh no." She shook her head violently. "To-*night*. You are writing and uploading that bad boy to Wattpad *tonight*," she told me. "Or those algebra equations? They'll be the *least* of your problems."

I snorted. "You know, if you're in *that* much of a hurry, you could always write the next chapter yourself."

"Wait, what?" She looked at me, puzzled. "What do you mean?"

"I don't know." I shrugged. I had meant it as a joke, but now that I thought about it, it wasn't actually a bad idea. "I mean, who says I have to be the only one writing this? Like, what if, from now on, we started taking turns? You write one chapter, then I'll write the next. That way we'll have double the story in half the time."

I wasn't 100 percent positive that the math added up—Madison was the math ninja in our little squad, not me—but it sounded good at any rate.

"Really? You'd let me do that?" Sarah's eyes shone with excitement. "'Cause I will totally do that! If you're serious. I mean, I'm definitely not as good of a writer as you are. But I know *exactly* what should happen next."

I hid a smile. "And what is that, may I ask?" Knowing Sarah, it would definitely be something featuring over-the-top romance.

She shot me a smug look. "Sorry, Smith. No spoilers." She reached over and grabbed the brownie off my plate, biting off half before returning it to my tray. "I guess you'll just have to find some other way to cling to life until tomorrow," she added, repeating my own words back to me with a smirk.

I sighed. "I've created a monster, haven't I?"

"You have no idea."

"You guys! Oh my gosh, you guys! You are literally not going to believe this!"

Sarah and I looked up from lunch just in time to see Kalani dive toward our table, her long black hair swishing from side to side as she clutched her cell phone in her hands. Technically we were supposed to keep our phones in our lockers during the day, but Kalani always seemed to find a way to skirt the stupid rule and not get caught. I, on the other hand, could have had a random stray thought about a phone and I'd probably be suspended for a month.

As Kalani plopped down into her seat—the one we saved for her every lunch period (as every lunch period she seemed to find a new and unique reason to be late)—Sarah and I leaned in, to see what it was we would "literally" not be able to believe this time around. With Kalani you never knew. It could be that someone had discovered the cure for cancer. Or that the caf was serving pizza tomorrow.

Or, in this particular case, something called Comicpalooza.

"Comic-pa-looza?" I read, scrunching up my face in question. "What's that?"

"*You* don't know?" Kalani raised an eyebrow. "Time to turn in your geek card, Smith."

I frowned, a little offended. "Hey, I live long and prosper like a boss, and don't you forget it."

"If that's true, then you should totally know about Comicpalooza," she declared. "It's, like, this huge international comic convention they hold every year in Houston. Kind of like Comic-Con in San Diego—but not quite as big. All these celebrities come and everyone dresses up in costumes and they have this huge floor where you can buy, like, a Harry Potter wand or a model *Millennium Falcon*."

"Okay . . ." I gave her a curious look, wondering why she was so excited about this.

I mean, don't get me wrong—it sounded super cool to me, the resident geek gamer of our group. But for Kalani to be this excited over something that was not pizza or Collin Prince (or Collin Prince eating pizza), there had to be something I was missing. "Well, that sounds great . . ."

"Though not all that unbelievable, if they hold it every year," Sarah added helpfully.

Kalani rolled her eyes, not dignifying her remark

with a response. Instead she pushed her phone into our faces again. This time my eyes caught something new: a small photo just beneath the large headline banner.

I gasped, my eyes widening. I looked up at Kalani. She bounced in her seat, grinning like a loon. "Told you!" she said triumphantly.

Plucking the phone from her grasp, I stared down at the screen. Stared down at the smiling face of none other than Collin Prince himself, listed under "Special Guests." I almost dropped the phone.

Collin Prince. Meeting fans.

Collin Prince. Signing autographs. Taking pictures.

Collin Prince reenacting his best magic tricks and stunts on stage in front of a live studio audience.

I swallowed hard, then looked up at my friends. For once, Kalani was right. I literally could not believe it.

"What's with you guys?"

We looked over to see our friend Madison heading in our direction to round out our foursome, her tray piled high with food. As the total jock of our little group, she was always going back for seconds. Sometimes thirds. According to her, being the star pitcher of one's softball team made one very hungry. Especially, it would seem in Madison's case, for multiple desserts. Seriously, if you looked up "sweet tooth" on Wikipedia, you'd probably find a photo of Madison's teeth.

I handed the phone to her without a word. Her blue eyes widened. She looked up and grinned. "Whoa," she said. "We have to go to this!"

"Exactly!" Kalani agreed. "That's what I was saying. Houston's only six hours away. He may never be this close to us again. And it's the first week of summer vacation, so we don't even have to worry about missing school."

"We *have* to go," Sarah declared, looking dreamily at my story again. "If we miss out on this, we might as well miss out on life itself."

Madison rolled her eyes at me from behind Sarah's back. In addition to being an actress onstage, Sarah had the reputation of being a bit of a drama queen in real life—and often her reactions could be over the top. But in this case I wasn't entirely sure she was exaggerating. This *was* a once-in-a-lifetime opportunity. We had to make it happen somehow.

Especially since . . .

My eyes locked onto the phone again. Under all the celebrity announcements there was also a little article about the convention's writers' track. Evidently there would be real-life authors attending as well as several editors, giving workshops and doing book signings.

But what really caught my eye? The announcement of a competition for young writers, sixteen and under, complete with prizes, including a hundred dollars in cash and a scholarship to a summer writing camp.

I gave a low whistle. A writing camp. How cool would that be? To spend my summer doing nothing but writing stories—with no chores to do, no parents to interrupt. It sounded like a dream come true.

I looked up at my friends. "Okay. It's settled," I said. "We're going."

They all nodded in agreement, probably assuming I was still thinking of Collin. And I was, of course. But the idea of winning the writing contest as well? Well, *that* would be the cherry on top of this delicious Comicpalooza sundae.

"Ooh! And we must cosplay, too!" Kalani declared. "According to my research, *everyone* dresses up at Comicpalooza. It's like Halloween times a gazillion."

My friends nodded in agreement. The four of us had always been into cosplay. Every Halloween we'd spurn the silly, cheap costumes-in-a-bag found at most stores and instead work to create elaborate ensembles cobbled together from things we found lying around the house or picked up at local craft stores. I'd even once created actual armor, using craft foam and metallic spray paint, to create a cosplay of my favorite character in the Fields of Fantasy video game, and I'd won first place in our town's annual Halloween costume contest.

But this . . . this was a step beyond. We'd really need to up our game if we were going to do this.

"Dibs on Zelda," I called out, probably unnecessarily. My friends—as much as I loved them—would probably not even recognize my favorite video game character if they ran into her on the street, never mind have the desire to dress as her in public. The armor Zelda wore would be difficult to make, but I was up for the challenge.

"Really? I thought you were going to say Rey from *Star Wars*," Sarah said. "After all, you look just like her."

"No, *I'm* going to do Rey," Madison butted in. "I may have blond hair, but I'm way more kick-butt than Hailey—no offense, Hailey—which is kind of a require-ment for our favorite Jedi. Not to mention I've always wanted my own lightsaber."

"Maybe you can get one of those stuffed BB-8, too," I suggested excitedly. "Have you seen them? They are *so* cute."

"Not as cute as my Pinkie Pie costume is going to be!" Kalani broke in, bouncing up and down. "Just call me the party pony, 'cause I will be bringing down the house at Comicpalooza!" She reached out and high-fived the group, slamming her hand against my own with such enthusiasm she almost knocked me off my chair.

She would make a great party pony.

"What about you, Sarah?" Madison asked. "What are you going to be?"

We all turned to look at her, waiting for her answer. But Sarah just smiled, reaching into her pocket to pull out her wallet. A moment later she produced the cut-out picture of Collin Prince she'd downloaded off the Web and printed out. Though we'd all seen this picture a thousand times before, we leaned in anyway, taking in his beautiful face. His deep brown eyes. His dark hair.

Sarah stroked the photo with her finger.

"If we're really going to the ball to meet the prince," she declared, "I will be going as a princess."

2

"SO WHAT DO YOU THINK?"

I hopped on one foot, then the other, as I waited with bated breath for my stepmother to finish reading the website. With my dad in China on business for the next three months, she was the only one I had to hit up.

She shook her head, letting out a low whistle. "Collin Prince," she said, almost under her breath. "Well, well, well. Who would have thought?"

"What do you mean who would have thought?" I demanded. "Do you even know who he is?" Let's just say that my stepmother, while thankfully not wicked, was not exactly hip, either, when it came to these kinds of things. So it surprised me to see what looked a lot like recognition flash across her face.

She looked up. "Of course I know who he is," she said with a laugh. "I used to be his teacher."

"Wait, *what*?" I stared at her, my heart thudding in my chest. "You were his *teacher*? Like his *real* teacher? Like you had him in class and you gave him homework and everything?"

She rolled her eyes. "Yes, Hailey. He's a local kid. Or he was, anyway, until his parents got divorced and he went to live with his dad in California. In any case, he went to Rollins, where I used to teach fifth grade. And yes, I even gave him homework. Which, I might add, he barely ever turned back in." She shook her head. "I swear, he had to have been one of the worst math students I ever had."

"Well, clearly he didn't need math," I pointed out, feeling a little offended on Collin's behalf. "Except maybe to count his millions and all."

I found myself staring down at her hands. Hands that had touched Collin Prince's homework. Of course, she'd probably done something stupid like washed them a thousand times since then.

Right then I made a solemn swear to myself. If I ever got the chance to touch Collin Prince's homework? There would be *no handwashing ever.*

I watched as my stepmother clicked on the website link that led from the Comicpalooza page to Collin's YouTube site. His latest video was one of the *Weird Foods You Should Not Stick Up Your Nose* series he'd been doing for the last few months. In this particular one he was stuffing wasabi up his nose while sweat poured down his face.

Okay, even I had to admit, it wasn't his magnum opus.

My stepmother shook her head. "Ten million people watched this?" she asked, her voice not disguising her astonishment.

"Ten million isn't even that many!" I protested. "He got at least fifteen million the time the not-on-fire guy dared him to skateboard off a roof into his neighbor's pool in seven seconds."

"I'm sorry I missed that one. . . ."

"Well, it's still online. You just have to click on the most watched—"

She laughed, holding up a hand in my direction. "I

think I'm good," she said in a voice that sounded way too condescending for my liking. "And I'm very . . . pleased . . . to see one of my former students making something of his life. Even if it is"—she turned back to the screen and shuddered a little—"spicy green snot."

I groaned. Of all videos, she'd had to pick that one. "He also does stunts," I protested. "And magic tricks. And he talks about . . . national important issue stuff too."

She gave me a vacant smile. I sighed.

"Look, I just want to go and meet him," I said. "That's all."

The smile slipped from her face. She turned back to the laptop, clicking to return to the Comicpalooza website. I sat there, my stomach churning. As if I had been the one to stick wasabi up my nose.

After what seemed an eternity, she turned back to me. "I'm sorry," she said. "I don't think that's going to be possible."

My heart dropped. For a moment I just sat there, hoping she was making a joke. A really horrible joke to torment me. But as the seconds ticked away, her expression didn't change. And something sank in my chest.

"Why not?" I demanded, once I'd found my voice.

"It's not even that far away. And it's the first week of summer vacation—so it doesn't interfere with school."

"It's six hours away," she corrected. "And a lot of money. Look. It's three hundred dollars for a VIP pass to meet him and attend his little show. Plus we'd have to stay in a hotel—for two nights—which would easily add another three hundred, minimum. Then there's gas to consider. A hundred bucks, easy." She shook her head. "That's a lot of money to spend on some kid who used to sleep through my class every day."

Oh my gosh! She got to see Collin Prince asleep? I nearly swooned at the thought, and it was all I could do not to demand complete, intricate intel on what his black lashes looked like, sweeping across his soft cheeks.

But, sadly, these vitally important details would have to wait for the universe to restore itself and justice to be served. I drew in a breath, trying to focus. Trying to sound adult.

"Look," I said, "I know he's just some random kid to you. But he's kind of the most important thing in my life. If I don't see him, I will pretty much die. And what will Dad say if he comes home to find a dead kid? I'm guessing that wouldn't do wonders for your marriage, right?"

She frowned, and I wondered if maybe I'd gone too far. After all, I knew it wasn't exactly easy for my stepmother to single-parent two kids when my dad was away for extended periods of time—especially when one of those kids wasn't even her own flesh and blood.

My mother had died of breast cancer when I was just a baby, and for most of my growing-up life it had been just Dad and me. Which, for the record, suited me just fine. But Dad could never get over the feeling that I needed a female role model in my life, and when I turned ten he started getting more and more serious about the dating scene. A new wife for him, he'd say, and a new mom for me. When he found my stepmother, who also came with the added "bonus" of a stepsibling for his only child, he proposed.

Of course, he'd had no idea at the time that his company would acquire a factory overseas that required long trips abroad. And I knew he felt horribly guilty on both ends—being forced to leave me and being forced to leave my stepmother stuck caring for me. To her credit, Nancy never complained. But sometimes she got this weird look in her eyes that told me this was not what she'd signed up for.

Like right now, for instance.

My stepmother sighed. "Sorry, kid. It's just not in the budget. Maybe next year." She started to rise to her feet. In desperation I grabbed her arm.

"But there isn't going to be a next year!" I protested, even while knowing I should just shut up right now and let it go. She clearly was not going to change her mind. And yet something inside me—some inner patheticism—compelled my mouth to keep moving. To keep begging. "It says right here: 'this year only'! If we miss 'this year only' . . ."

Tell her about the writing contest, a voice inside me nagged. But somehow the words got stuck in my throat. I'd never told her about my writing. And if I told her now, she'd want to read it. And what if she read it and thought it wasn't any good? What if she told me I shouldn't enter the contest—because I didn't have a chance to win? Sure, my friends liked my fan fiction. But they would like anything that involved Collin Prince. Even snotty wasabi. My stepmom, on the other hand, was a teacher. She probably read good writing all the time.

And while it was awful to be denied Comicpalooza on the account of money, it would be even worse if she told me I shouldn't bother—because I was too terrible to even try.

"I'm sorry, Hailey." She gave me a frustrated look. "I'm not trying to be mean here. But with your dad away and me only substitute teaching . . . well, we don't have a lot of extra money to blow on this kind of thing."

"What if I didn't eat for three months? You could save the money you would normally spend on food."

She snorted. "Then your father *would* come home to a dead kid."

"I mean, I would eat *something*." Seriously, why was she so determined to shoot down my every idea without even thinking it through? "Like ramen noodles. They're super cheap. And peanut butter and jelly sandwiches." I gave her my best pleading look. "Please, Nancy. Don't do this to me!"

She rose to her feet, shaking off my hand. "I said no, Hailey. And I need you to respect my decision."

"Even if your decision stinks?"

A shadow crossed her face. *Uh-oh.*

"I think you need to go to your room," she said in a quiet voice. "Until you're able to calm down and reset that attitude." She paused, her steely blue eyes locking onto me. "Or do you need me to call your father and wake him up in China to talk about it?"

I slumped back in my chair, knowing I'd lost. Playing the dad card—well, that was her ace in the hole every time. "No, you don't need to call Dad," I muttered. "I'll let you trample on my hopes and dreams without running up the long-distance bill. Which we clearly can't afford to do."

She gave me a weary look. "I'm sorry, sweetheart," she said. "Someday when you get a job, you can choose what you want to spend your money on," she told me. "But for now, you're going to have to deal with the budget our family has made. And right now there's no room in that budget for YouTube stars."

3

"THERE'S NO ROOM IN THAT BUDGET FOR YOUTUBE STARS,'"
I mimicked in my most sarcastic voice as I stuck my finger down my throat, pretending to vomit. I paced the room, my steps eating up the distance between walls. I looked over at my friends. "Seriously, she always pretends to be this sweet, nice stepmother, rocking against the cliché. But clearly she has the evil gene deep down in her DNA, just waiting for the right moment to strike." I made a face. "And of course she picks *this* moment. The worst possible moment ever."

Madison, Sarah, and Kalani gave me matching sympathetic looks from where they sat on Madison's bed. We had gathered here together, as per usual, for our weekly Collin Prince fan club meeting. But we hadn't even watched any of his new videos yet. We were all way too depressed.

"My mom pretty much said the exact same thing," Sarah said miserably. "I believe the phrase 'waste of money' came out of her mouth at one point."

"What is *wrong* with parents?" Kalani demanded. "It is literally *not* a waste of money. In fact, it's a waste of life *not* to spend money on something so epic. I mean, when we die, are we going to remember food? Clothing? Shelter? No. We are going to remember the day we missed out on seeing Collin Prince—that's what we're going to remember."

"Totally," Madison agreed. "My parents have tons of money and they still said no. Something about being too busy to waste a weekend on some teenybopper fantasy— whatever that's supposed to mean."

I flopped down on Madison's bed and stared up at her canopy. Her mother, a professional interior designer, had woven rustic brown branches around the poles, then added yellow LED lights, making it look like you were inside a magical fairy forest every time you lay down in bed. I always thought it was the coolest thing ever, even if it made Madison roll her eyes.

However, today even twinkling lights couldn't boost my bad mood. "I hate money," I said with a sigh. "All it does is cause problems."

"I would be happy to have those kinds of problems," Sarah said. "Seriously—I would be the best rich person ever, if someone would just give me a chance."

"I know, right?" I agreed. "I wouldn't even mind working for it. The day I turn fourteen, I am joining the workforce and I am never looking back."

"You know, we could try to raise the money ourselves," Sarah said suddenly, sitting up in bed.

"How would we do that?" Kalani asked.

She shrugged. "I don't know. We could . . . hold a bake sale?"

"No offense, but I've tasted your cookies," I said. "No one's going to bite."

"True." She pursed her lips. "Delivering newspapers, maybe? Like a . . . paper girl?"

"Who gets newspapers delivered anymore? Everyone's online."

She groaned. "Well, then, how much do you get for giving blood? Or . . . bone marrow? Isn't that a thing?"

"Hold on," Madison interjected suddenly, sitting

up in bed. "As much as I'd be willing and happy to donate bodily fluids to the Collin Prince cause, I just got a less . . . invasive idea."

We all turned to her expectantly.

"We could babysit," she said. "My sister babysits practically every weekend. She gets paid, like, ten dollars an hour to sit around and eat popcorn and watch bad movies."

"Whoa. My goal in *life* is to get paid to eat snacks and watch bad movies!" Kalani declared. "How does one get in on this babysitting action?"

"Do you have to be fourteen?" Sarah asked doubtfully.

"I don't think there's, like, a rule about it," I mused.

"But we can't drive. How would we get to the jobs?"

"We could walk to a lot of them," I said. "Or ride our bikes. I mean, think of all the families in our subdivision alone—that's a lot of potential jobs within walking distance."

"And I'm sure our parents will drive us to the ones that are farther out," added Madison.

"Or my brother could," Kalani said. "He just got his license and is dying for an excuse to use the car."

"What about curfews? My mom would flip if I was out late on school nights," Sarah pointed out.

"Right, but a lot of moms need after-school care," I reminded her. "And then we could still offer later nights on weekends—if we needed extra money."

"Let's see. If each of us babysat six hours a week for the next two months . . ." Madison banged on her phone's calculator. "At ten dollars an hour . . . for eight weeks . . ." She looked up. "That's more than nineteen hundred dollars."

"We'd need twelve hundred for everyone to get a Collin Prince VIP pass," I said, doing the math in my head. "And three hundred for two nights in a hotel—we can all cram into one room, right? I don't mind sleeping on the floor. And my stepmom estimated a hundred dollars in gas."

Kalani turned to Madison. "How much is that, oh mighty math ninja?"

"Sixteen hundred," she replied, without even using her calculator. Not that I was jealous or anything.

"Which would leave us three hundred for food and souvenirs," concluded Sarah. She looked up at us, a big grin spreading across her face. "Which would be more than enough!"

We stared at one another, our eyes widening, for a moment unable to move. Could this actually work?

Could we really make enough money on our own to finance the trip?

Kalani moved first, leaping to her feet and bouncing on the bed excitedly. "We're gonna meet Collin Prince!" she crowed. She bounded over to the poster Madison had hung on the wall and gave Collin a loud smacking kiss. "I am literally going to do that in person when I see you!" she promised his picture.

I grabbed her hand and yanked her back down onto the bed. "First of all, I'm going to take a wild guess and say kissing privileges aren't part of the VIP experience," I said. "And second, you might want to hold off on launching into a full-on victory celebration just yet. We do actually have to earn this hypothetical money first."

"True," Madison agreed. "Babysitting for six hours a week will only happen if we can find parents who want to hire us."

"Yeah. Good luck with *that*."

We looked up, surprised. We'd been so involved in our calculations we hadn't heard Madison's older sister, Jordan, accompanied by my stepsister, Ginny, walk into the room. They surveyed us now, matching smug expressions on their faces.

I scowled. "What's that supposed to mean?" I demanded.

"Are you kidding me?" Ginny cried. "You think anyone's going to hire you tools to watch their kids? You've barely graduated from having babysitters yourselves."

"We're thirteen," Madison shot back defensively. "According to US federal law we are totally legal to babysit." She held out her phone to show off her Google research to prove it.

Jordan and Ginny exchanged knowing looks. "Well, then," Jordan said with a sniff. "I guess if it's legal, that makes it all okay."

"Though good luck getting any jobs," Ginny added with a snort.

"Why wouldn't we?" I demanded.

She shrugged. "Please. We've got this neighborhood locked up tight. The parents know us. They love us. And you've got no way to compete with that except with inferior age and less experience." She gave us a mean smile.

"But hey—don't let us stop you from trying," Jordan chimed in. "By all means, put out some flyers. Post around the Web. I'm sure parents will be jumping to let a bunch of random kids they've never heard of take care of their precious brats."

I scowled back at her. I wanted to tell her she didn't know what she was talking about, but at the same time I wasn't sure she was wrong. Why *would* someone hire us over experienced, older babysitters like Ginny and Jordan? What did we have to offer that they didn't already offer better?

"Why do you even want to babysit so badly, anyway?" Jordan asked her sister. "After all, you've got your whole lives ahead of you to work. Why not enjoy your youth while you can? Go to the pool. The mall. The movies."

"But then we wouldn't get to see Collin Prince," Kalani protested.

"Collin Prince?" Ginny shot Jordan a curious look before turning back to us. "Where are you going to see Collin Prince?"

"Nowhere," I said quickly, after shooting Kalani a warning look. The last thing we needed was to give these two more ammunition. "Now, if you're finished, we're actually kind of busy here. . . ."

But, like it or not, we'd gotten their full attention now. Jordan grabbed the iPad off her sister's bed and scanned the screen. She looked up at Ginny.

"He's going to be in Houston," she said excitedly.

Ginny peered over her shoulder at the iPad. "Comic-PAH-loser?" she read, squinting at the screen. "What's that?"

"Nothing. Just some nerd thing you wouldn't understand," I tried, working to wrestle the iPad back. But Jordan had a death grip and wouldn't let go.

"Collin Prince isn't a nerd," she pointed out. She turned to Ginny. "We should go to this."

Ugh. I cringed. It was the last thing I wanted to happen. Not to mention totally unfair. They didn't even like geeky things. In fact, Ginny had pretty much made it her life's mission to torment me over my *Doctor Who* obsession and video game marathons.

Of all people, they didn't deserve to go to Comicpalooza. And they certainly didn't deserve to meet Collin Prince.

But unfortunately, they had one thing we didn't have: cash to spend. And Jordan had a car, so really, two things. Two very important things. The two *most* important things, if we were being technical here.

I sighed. I *really* didn't want to do this. I really, *really* didn't want to do this. But desperate times and all that. And if swallowing my pride meant an actual chance to see Collin Prince and enter the writing contest to boot, well, I'd choke it down without water and smile.

"If you do go," I said meekly, "can we come too?"

Jordan burst out laughing. She looked at my friends and me, scorn radiating from her eyes. "You've got to be kidding, right?" she asked incredulously. "You think we'd take you dorks out in public with us? To meet Collin Prince?" She turned to Ginny and snorted loudly. "Knowing them, they'd probably show up in costume."

"That's not weird at Comicpalooza, actually," Madison tried.

"Like, literally, everyone will be in costume," Kalani muttered under her breath.

Jordan rolled her eyes. "Fine," she said. "Whatever. If you can somehow manage to save up enough money to go, then I suppose we can stomach you along for the ride. But you have to promise you will not try to hang out with us once we get there. Like, zero contact until it's time to go home."

I nodded. Now *that* was a promise I'd have no problem keeping.

"It's a deal," I told her. "And we *will* get the money. You just wait and see."

Ginny gave me a smirk. "I'll be holding my breath," she assured me. Then she turned to Jordan. "Let's go. The reek of desperation is clogging my nasal passages."

And with that, the two of them sauntered out of the room. Madison leaped off the bed to slam the door behind them. She returned a moment later, looking extremely annoyed.

"Sisters," she muttered, glancing over at me.

"Stepsisters," I agreed. I guess I could be grateful at least mine wasn't a blood relative.

"They're just jealous," Sarah declared. "They know in their hearts that at thirteen we're already way cooler than they'll ever be."

"Imagine how stupid they're going to look at Comicpalooza," Kalani scoffed. "They are going to stick out like sore thumbs."

"Sore thumbs with money," I pointed out dismally. "And unfortunately, they're not wrong about the babysitting thing. How *are* we going to get anyone to hire us? We've got nothing to offer to make parents pick us instead of them."

"Which is so not fair." Madison lay back on her bed, staring up at the fairy canopy. "Why should they get all the good babysitting jobs just 'cause they're older? Age doesn't make you a good babysitter."

"Right? All Ginny used to do when she babysat me was sit me in front of the TV while she texted her boyfriend all night," I said. "I bet she does the same thing now. Doesn't even play with the kids."

"I would totally play with the kids if I was babysitting." Kalani screwed up her face in disgust. "That's literally what you're getting paid to do, right?"

"Exactly," Madison agreed. "Well, that and keep the kids safe and all. But we could do that, too. Like playing games *and* keeping your kids safe—two services for the price of one!" She shrugged. "Not that we could probably put that on the flyer or anything."

Sarah sighed. "I used to have the best babysitter ever," she remembered. "She would bring over all these amazing costumes. For both of us. And we'd play all these crazy made-up games, like Princess in the Castle, until it was time for me to go to bed. I always thought if I became a babysitter someday, I'd want to be just like her."

"She sounds amazing," I said.

"She was. In fact, she was so amazing she ended up

starting her own princess party company to help fund her college tuition."

"What's a princess party company?" Kalani asked.

"It's like, if your kid loves Cinderella, you pay this company and they send over a Cinderella for their birthday—all dressed up and in character—to entertain the kids," Sarah explained. "Usually they have games and sing-alongs and they help cut the cake. It's pretty awesome. My younger cousin had a princess party when she turned four. Let's just say the kids were freaking out when a certain snow queen *let it go*, right there in the middle of the living room."

She grabbed the iPad and pulled up a website. We leaned in to check it out. Sure enough, there were all these pictures of girls who looked just like princesses, playing with groups of excited kids. It looked super fun. And getting paid to dress up in costume? That was even cooler than the free-snacks-and-watching-TV thing.

And then . . . suddenly I got an idea.

A really awesome idea.

A really awesome, totally doable idea . . .

I looked up at my friends, my heart pounding in my chest with excitement. This could be the competitive edge we were looking for. The thing that set us apart from the Ginnys and Jordans of the world. The niche that would make parents want to hire us over any other babysitters. Because we wouldn't be like the other boring old babysitters.

Or, at the very least, we wouldn't look like them.

"We could totally do this!" I burst out.

"What?" My friends glanced over at me, confused looks on their faces.

"You want us to start a princess party company?" asked Madison.

"No." I shook my head, a smile stretching across my face. "I want to start a princess *babysitting* company."

4

MY FRIENDS ALL STARED AT ME. I GRINNED WIDELY.

"We need a competitive edge, right? Over the other babysitters in the neighborhood?" I explained. "After all, they're older. They're more experienced. So of course parents are going to choose them over us. *Unless...*" I ran over to Madison's closet and whipped it open. "We give them ..." I shuffled through some of the clothes, then frowned. "Um, Madison? Do you even own a dress?"

She jumped off the bed and pushed her way to the very back of her closet until all I could see were her tennis shoes, sticking out. "I think ... there ... might be ... one ... here ... somewhere...." She grunted and pushed farther back until she disappeared from sight. (Seriously, did she have Narnia stashed back there?) Kalani and Sarah looked at me skeptically as I proceeded to lose all my momentum.

"Aha!" Madison cried triumphantly. She emerged from the closet with an atrocious-looking straggly pink thing on a hanger. It was sparkly. It was fur-trimmed. And it was *so* un-Madison that we all burst out laughing. She frowned at us, shoving the dress in my direction.

"What?" she growled. "My aunt still thinks I'm six, okay?"

I was pretty sure even a six-year-old would barf at this particular frothy, frilly monstrosity, but it would have to do. I held up the dress in front of me, then turned to my friends, pasting a huge smile on my face.

"Hi, kids! I'm Princess Hailey—so great to meet you! I've come all the way from my kingdom in the clouds to play with you tonight. Isn't that so exciting? Aren't I so much cooler than all those boring old babysitters your mother usually sticks you with?" I took a step forward, reaching out my hand . . .

"Mommy! Don't leave me with the furry pink monster!" Kalani screamed. "I think she's going to eat me!" She play-cowered behind Sarah and then burst out laughing.

I rolled my eyes, tossing the sorry excuse for a dress back into the closet. "Okay, fine. Clearly we'd need to up our costume game."

"And work on less creepy meet-and-greets," Sarah added dryly.

"Yes, yes," I agreed. "But think about the big picture here. Think about what an amazing hook this will be. We show up to all our babysitting gigs dressed as beautiful princesses and totally in character, too. As far as the little kids know, we're the real deal, coming to spend a magical evening with them. It'll be just like the princesses who do the parties—same games and all that—but for one or two special little kids each night. They will totally love it!"

"And the parents will love it too," Sarah said thoughtfully, nodding her head. "They pay big bucks for those princess parties. So this could be, like, a big savings. A princess for the price of a babysitter."

"Yeah, but shouldn't we charge extra?" Madison asked. "We would be going through a lot more trouble than if we just showed up in jeans and a T-shirt. We're talking extreme makeover anytime we have a gig."

"No." I shook my head. "We charge exactly the same.

Then they can't use the idea of trying to save money as an excuse not to hire us. They can either have someone boring like Jordan or Ginny. Or, for the exact same price, they can have us!"

"What about boys?" Sarah asked. "Are we limiting ourselves to the girl market here?"

"Some boys like princesses," Kalani pointed out. "I saw this thing online where a boy wanted to be Elsa for Halloween and his dad totally let him do it. He rocked that dress, too, I might add."

"Yeah, but most boys aren't like that," Madison interjected. "And not all girls like princesses, either. When I was four and my parents tried to force Snow White on me at Disney World, I kicked her so hard I left a bruise." She grinned, remembering. "That was when they finally gave in and took me to Pirates of the Caribbean. I even got a pirate makeover!"

She hopped off her bed, dashed to her dresser, and grabbed a pirate hat that had been hanging from the mirror. She tossed it on her head and turned to face us, a fierce snarl on her face.

"Arrr . . . me mateys! Any of you scallywags be wantin' to walk the plank?"

"Only if young Johnny Depp is at the end of it," Sarah muttered.

My eyes widened. "That's perfect!" I cried. "We could totally do that."

"Make young Johnny Depp walk the plank?" Kalani asked, confused.

"That, unfortunately, may be beyond even our powers," I said. "But we could create a babysitting company featuring princesses *and* pirates. It could be, like, kids' choice."

My friends looked at one another, nodding thoughtfully.

"I like it," Sarah said.

"It could totally work," agreed Kalani.

"And we could call the company Princesses and Pirates . . . Incorporated," Madison finished. "It has a nice ring to it."

I felt a grin spreading across my face. It did have a nice ring to it. The kind of ring that would hopefully make the phone ring with tons of babysitting jobs.

"Just think," I said. "We'd get to do something we already all love—cosplay—and we'd get to make money from it at the same time! It's perfect!"

"It is more than perfect!" Kalani crowed. She held up her hands, inviting more of her famous high fives. This time none of us held back. "It's literally the best idea ever."

And it kind of was, I thought as I slapped my hand against my friends'. We could rock this new company. We could line up babysitting gigs all spring long. We could make money hand over fist.

And come summer vacation, we could hit the road. To see our Prince at last.

I so needed to start working on my new writing project if I was going to be ready.

5

"So . . . what do you think?" I asked, presenting the newly printed flyer to my friends at lunch Monday. They passed it to one another, reading it over, then looked up at me.

"It's perfect!" Sarah declared. "Absolutely perfect."

"People are going to be bending over backward to give us babysitting jobs," added Madison. "I call dibs on the first pirate request!"

"We're going to have more jobs than we know what to do with!" crowed Kalani, rubbing her hands together in excitement.

I smiled, feeling very pleased. "Okay," I said. "I'm going to get a bunch of these printed out in the computer lab, then go around tonight and hang them up in the neighborhood. At the playgrounds, the mailbox areas. Anywhere parents might hang out."

"I can hang them around the softball fields after practice," Madison said. "There's always tons of parents with little kids there."

"I can post stuff on Facebook," Kalani added. "There's that new neighborhood group everyone's on. They're always looking for babysitters."

"Ooh, and maybe we can hit up the local newspaper?"

Sarah suggested. "Get them to do an article on us or whatever?"

"Let's get a few jobs under our belts first," I said. "Make sure we've really got this before we alert the media."

"Yeah, we don't even have any princess or pirate costumes yet," Madison pointed out. "Maybe that's something we need to talk about before the flyers."

"Agreed. Normally I'd say we should make our own like we do for our other cosplays," I said. "But we need to get started sooner rather than later if we're going to have enough time to make the money we need by the end of May."

"Ooh! I almost forgot!" Sarah burst out. "Mee-Maw said we could use her attic!"

We all looked at her, puzzled.

"Don't you remember? My grandmother used to be an actress!" she reminded us. "And she has all these wardrobes and chests up in her attic, just full of costumes. I used to raid them all the time when I was a kid. Of course, they didn't fit me back then. But now . . . all we have to do is go up there and pick out what we want and she'll let us borrow them."

"That's great!" I exclaimed. "Then we'd only have to buy the pirate costumes." I turned to the group. "Okay. Today is flyer day—I really want to get the word out. Then tomorrow we'll raid Sarah's grandmother's attic after school." I smiled at my friends. "Sound like a plan?"

Everyone nodded in agreement just as the bell rang, announcing it was time to head back to class. As I accompanied Sarah to return my tray, she turned to me, giving me an expectant look.

"So where is it?" she asked.

I frowned. "Where is what?"

"The next chapter, of course!" she cried. "It was your turn, remember? I did yesterday's!"

Uh-oh. I bit my lower lip. I had been so busy last night, working on the flyer, I'd completely forgotten I owed her a new chapter in the Collin Prince story.

Okay, fine. I hadn't *completely*, completely forgotten. It was just . . . homework had taken a long time, and when I'd finally finished, I'd really wanted to work on my more important project: the story for the Comicpalooza writer's contest.

But I couldn't exactly tell *her* that. She would flip out if she knew I was working on something new, now that she was cowriting the sensational Collin Prince saga. In fact, she'd probably say something crazy like I should enter *that* story into the competition. Which was, of course, ridiculous. The story was fun, after all. But definitely not prizewinning literature.

Not that I could say that to her. At least not without sounding insulting.

I realized she was still staring at me, waiting for an answer. I barked out what I hoped was a casual laugh. "Oh my gosh!" I cried. "I can't believe I forgot to bring it to school."

Her eyes narrowed suspiciously. "So it's written?" she asked. "It's just . . . home?"

"I'll email it the *second* I get home," I promised. "So you won't have to wait."

"Oh, fine." She pretended to pout. "I suppose I can wait that long. But you'd better have that bad boy up before dinner," she added. "Or I am coming to your house and stealing it from your bedroom."

My stomach squirmed. "No need," I assured her. "It'll be up. I promise."

Guess I knew what I'd be working on this study hall.

* * *

And so I found myself, later that afternoon, canvassing the neighborhood on my bike with my newly printed flyers. I hit up all the mailbox stations and the three playgrounds and I was just working on the rec center when I heard a voice behind me.

"Are kids really bored of babysitters?"

I whirled around, my eyes widening as they fell on a boy around my age straddling a silver bicycle. It took me a moment to recognize him as Brody, the new kid at school who had just joined my pre-algebra class.

In class he sat at the opposite end of the room from me, so I hadn't been able to get a good look at him up until now. He was tall, with curly brown hair that hung a bit too long into his eyes, and he wore ripped jeans with a pair of gray Converse on his feet. But what really got my attention was his shirt—with the Legend of Zelda Tri-Force symbol emblazoned on the front.

So he was a gamer. Interesting.

I realized he was waiting for an answer. "Um, some kids might be bored," I said with a shrug, feeling a little sheepish. "Though I didn't, like, do an official study on it or anything. . . ."

He didn't reply. Just dismounted his bike and kicked

out the kickstand, then headed in my direction and plucked the flyer from my hand.

"Princess babysitting?" He looked up. "Is that a thing?"

I felt my face heat, though I wasn't sure why. "It's *going* to be a thing," I told him. "My friends and I are starting our own company."

"Where you dress up as princesses and go babysitting?"

"Yeah." I shrugged. "Or pirates. I mean, we haven't actually done it yet, but that's the plan."

"Cool." To my surprise, instead of returning the flyer, he took the tape out of my other hand and proceeded to hang it up for me on the bulletin board. I watched, shuffling from foot to foot, feeling like I should say something but having no idea what to say.

"We're just trying to make some money," I blurted out at last, feeling even more lame. 'Cause, duh, why else would you start a babysitting company? For your health?

He turned to me, handing me back the tape. "What for?" he asked.

"Wh-what?"

"You said you're trying to make money. Is it for something in particular?"

"Oh. Um . . ." I swallowed hard, my mind racing for something cool to say, but coming up blank. Of course I could tell him the truth—about Collin Prince—but it just suddenly seemed kind of embarrassing. What if he thought Collin Prince was lame? Most boys thought he was cool, but not all. And if he did think Collin Prince was lame, would he think I was lame for wanting to spend all that money to go see him?

Suddenly I remembered. "There's this writing thing," I blurted out. "At this comic convention in Houston in June."

"You mean Comicpalooza?"

My eyes widened. "You know about Comicpalooza?"

"Sure. I used to live in Houston before I moved here. I've been every year with my dad. He's an author and he signs books and speaks on panels and stuff."

I stared at him. His dad was an actual author? Like published and everything? That was the coolest thing ever!

"I want to be an author someday too," I told him, feeling a little sheepish about admitting it. "Which is why I want to enter this writing contest they're having. It's for kids under sixteen and the winner gets a scholarship to a summer writing camp."

"Summer writing camp? That sounds cool. I mean, I'm not a writer or anything, but if I was, I'd totally want to do something like that."

"Right? Of course, I need to save up enough money to get to Comicpalooza if I even want to enter. It's not cheap with the hotel and everything."

Brody nodded. "Well, I think that's a very noble goal," he said with a grin. A really cute grin, I might add, not that I was noticing. "And here I'm just trying to scrounge up enough money to buy a new PlayStation."

"Oh? Do you not have one?"

He sighed. "My old one completely burned out on me, and my parents refused to buy me a new one. I think somehow they believe I was careless with my old one, which I totally wasn't." He shot me a sheepish look. "Though I may have played it too much. . . ."

"Is that even possible?"

"I don't know." He shook his head. "In any case, it's dumb. And nothing compared to what you're saving up for. But I was right in the middle of the new Fields of Fantasy single-player game when it happened. My poor character probably thinks I abandoned him in that tavern forever."

"You play Fields of Fantasy?" I cried, before I could stop myself.

"You *know* Fields of Fantasy?" he countered, raising an eyebrow.

I frowned. "I happen to be a level-ninety fury warrior, thank you very much."

"That's . . . awesome," he declared, looking extremely impressed. (As well he should have been—it was quite an accomplishment, not to brag or anything.) "And I'm sorry. It's just, most girls look at me like I'm speaking a foreign language when I talk about video games."

"Well, lucky for you, I happen to speak fluent gamer. In fact . . ." I reached into my pocket and pulled out my phone, then scrolled through my photos until I found the ones from last Halloween. "Check it out."

He peered down at my phone and let out a low whistle. "That's you?" he asked. "Where did you get that costume? I've never seen anything from Fields of Fantasy in the stores. And that armor is totally sweet."

I grinned. "I made it."

"What?" He looked up, amazement clear in his eyes. I felt my cheeks heat a little. "You *made* it?"

"Yeah. My friends and I are really into cosplay. That's

one of the reasons we decided to do the babysitting thing to begin with. We figured we could put our costuming talents to good use and make some money."

"I don't suppose you're looking for more babysitters, are you?"

"You want to be a pirate?" I asked, surprised.

"I was thinking princess, actually. I happen to look ah-MAZ-ing in a pair of stilettos." He grinned. "And you should see the way I rock a petticoat."

I burst out laughing. "Mm-hm. I bet."

"Okay, fine." He waved his hand. "If I must be a pirate, then I guess I could do that, too."

He looked at me. He looked so hopeful it made me feel bad. I didn't want to disappoint him—after all, I could only imagine how much it would stink to have your favorite game console break down. But my friends would kill me if I added a random person to our little company. We needed all the money we could get by the end of the school year. Bringing on Brody would turn our four-way split into a five.

"Sorry," I said. "We're kind of full up at the moment."

He sighed. "Yeah, I figured. Though for the record,

I really *would* put on a dress in exchange for a new PlayStation."

I laughed. "And I'm sure you'd look marvelous in it," I teased. "But in the meantime, you're welcome to come over and play mine, if you ever find yourself in need of a fix."

He looked up. "Really?"

"Um, sure. If you wanted to. At some point. And, uh, I could show you how to make some of that armor, too, if you were interested."

Even as the words came from my mouth, I couldn't believe I was saying them. Had I really just gone and invited a cute boy over to my house to play video games and see my cosplay? I mean, what if he thought it was like a date? Did I want it to be like a date? Could playing video games even be considered a date? I had never been on one, of course, so I had no idea how these things worked, except what I'd seen on TV. And you never saw people playing video games on dates on TV. Never mind making armor.

His eyes met mine. And I noticed, for the first time, how blue they were. Like, not just the watery, washed-out blue of most eyes. But this crazy navy color, like he'd just walked out of my favorite anime.

"That'd be awesome, actually," he said. "If you're sure it'd be okay."

Gulp. Swallow. "Sure. I'm sure it would be great! Really great."

Ohmigosh. Ohmigosh.

As I stood there, pretty much frozen in place, wild butterflies doing the conga in my stomach, he reached out and plucked a few more flyers from my hand.

"I have to pass the pool on my way home," he said. "I can hang up a few over there if you want. Save you the trip."

"Oh. Great. That would be . . . great."

Seriously, Hailey. How many times are you going to use the word "great"?

"Um, thank you."

"Arr . . . It be my pleasure, me matey!" he growled, giving me a roguish wink. Then he laughed, holding up his hands in innocence. "Sorry. Not trying to change your mind or anything," he said, taking a step backward. He grinned. "Well, maybe just a little . . ."

And with that, before I could find the words to reply, he got back on his bike and rode down the street.

6

"WHOA! IT'S A LITTLE DUSTY UP HERE, ISN'T IT?"

Kalani sneezed loudly three times as we climbed the steps into Sarah's grandmother's attic the next afternoon, prompting Sarah to shoot her an annoyed look.

"It's an attic," she snapped. "What did you expect? Be lucky there's no ghosts."

Madison grinned at Kalani. "At least none that we know of . . ."

She cackled maniacally as Sarah pushed open the door that led into the attic, and Kalani scurried behind me, as if I'd be able to protect her from any random wandering spirits. She'd been deathly afraid of ghosts ever since her parents took her to Disney World and forced her to ride the Haunted Mansion ride when she was an impressionable three-year-old. (Which was ridiculous, since that ride is not even remotely scary.)

This attic, on the other hand, I had to admit, *was* pretty creepy. Cobwebs hung from the rafters, and there was no real floor, only crisscrossed wooden beams. A whistling noise purred from a darkened corner, which I told myself was, of course, the wind.

Even though it was not, actually, that windy a day . . .

"So, uh, dresses!" I suggested in my most cheerful voice as my eyes darted around the space. "Let's get those dresses!"

From the corner of my eye I could see Madison stifling her own sneeze into her sleeve, clearly not wanting to offend Sarah further. Sarah was very protective of her mee-maw, who had evidently been some big actress in the 1960s, though none of us had ever heard of her or any of her movies. Not that we would admit that to Sarah, of course—she probably would have forced us to sit through some kind of movie marathon in retaliation for not recognizing Mee-Maw's obvious celebrity.

In any case, right now we needed dresses. And if the woman was willing to lend her wardrobe to our cause,

I was fully prepared to become a Mee-Maw superfan for life.

"Here we are!" Sarah declared, sweeping her hand across the space. "The legendary attic of the legendary actress and songwriter Patty Greenberg."

I squinted a few times, trying to get my eyes adjusted to the dim lighting as I prepared to ooh and aah over all the beautiful princess dresses that would soon be revealed.

Except . . . there were no beautiful princess dresses— at least not at first glance. In fact, the attic seemed almost as empty as it was spooky.

"So, uh. . ." Kalani peeked out from behind me. "Where is everything?"

Sarah frowned, looking around. "Um . . ." she said.

"Maybe your mee-maw downsized her dresses over the years and then forgot she did?"

"Or maybe they were stolen by the ghosts," Madison suggested with a smirk, giving Kalani an evil stare. She gave a small *eep* and sank back behind me.

I rolled my eyes. "Or *maybe* they're all in that chest." I pointed to the large leather-bound monstrosity at the very far end of the attic.

Sarah looked relieved. "Yes," she said. "I'm sure that's

it! Come on." She stepped onto a thin wooden board and started making her way precariously to the chest. She looked like a gymnast crossing on a balance beam, and I wondered what would happen if she slipped. Would she crash through the floor like people always did when crossing attics in the movies?

"Be careful," I called to her. The last thing we needed was a princess babysitter with a broken leg.

"I got it. Don't worry."

I watched as she reached the chest and dropped to her knees, positioning her hands to yank on the handle. Unfortunately, it didn't budge.

"Maybe a ghost is sitting on it!" Madison suggested. Kalani whimpered.

"Can I get some help over here?" Sarah grunted.

It took a few minutes for us all to make the trip over, and at one point I was positive I was going to slip and fall, causing this adventure to be over before it ever really began. But somehow we managed to make it to the large piece of plywood that served as flooring at the end of the attic and positioned ourselves to help Sarah with the chest.

"On the count of three," she said. "One, two . . ."

On three we pushed hard, working together to inch

open the rusty lid. It wasn't easy—clearly whatever *was* inside this chest hadn't seen the light of day in quite a few years. But at last it gave way, creaking loudly as it swung open. (The sound caused Kalani to almost jump out of her skin.) I dropped my hands, wriggling my shoulders to stretch them out after the workout I'd just put them through, then prepared, once again, to ooh and aah over the treasure inside.

We all peered into the chest. Which, it turned out, was nearly empty. Oh dear.

"Um, that's it?" Kalani asked.

"Maybe there's, like, a key at the bottom that will unlock a real dress closet somewhere else in the house?" Madison suggested. "I read something like that in a mystery novel once. Of course, the killer was also hiding inside and—"

I shot her a warning look before she set Kalani off again. Not to mention, Sarah's face was quite pinched at this point.

"It's the quality, not the quantity," she muttered, rummaging through the box.

Madison grabbed a dark blue dress and held it up. "The quality of being eaten by moths?"

As if in response, a few moths fluttered out from one of the holey sleeves. Kalani shrieked and dropped the dress she had picked up like it was a hot potato, diving behind me again.

Sarah scowled. "It's just a few holes," she protested. "No one's even going to notice."

"No one's going to notice the princess they hired to watch their children looks like a homeless person?" Madison demanded, reaching in to pull a second dress from the chest. This one had some kind of tacky gold fringe that had come half unstitched dangling from the collar, and it was missing at least six buttons.

Sarah grabbed it from her, ripping off the fringe angrily. "As if your grandmother has anything half as nice."

"Are you kidding me? My grandmother is a vice president of Frost Bank. She wears Chanel suits on casual Friday. She wouldn't be caught dead in these bag-lady ball gowns."

Sarah's face was now approximately the same shade as a rotten eggplant. I jumped in between them before she could say something she was likely to regret.

"Look," I tried to interject, "these are all really

beautiful. And if we had more time, we could totally fix them up to be the best princess dresses ever. But we need dresses now. And, well, that means no time for major alterations."

"So what do you expect us to do?" demanded Sarah. "We can't exactly go out and buy new dresses. We're trying to make money here, not lose money."

I ran a hand through my hair, my thoughts whirring at a desperate pace. They were all looking at me, expecting me to have some kind of answer.

Then, suddenly, it hit me.

"Thrift shop," I said.

"What?"

"The other day, when I was talking to my stepmom. She was packing up all these clothes to send to the thrift shop."

"Um, we need princess dresses. Not mom jeans."

"Exactly. And what is the one day all moms dress up as princesses?" I asked. When they stared at me with blank faces, I groaned. "Their wedding day!"

"I don't get it," Kalani said.

"Have you ever seen a wedding dress?" I asked. "It's basically a princess dress in white."

"Right. In white. What, are we supposed to all be princess brides?" Madison asked.

"No. But we can dye the dresses."

Their eyes widened.

"Can you do that? I mean, is that even legal?" Kalani demanded.

"Why not? If we buy them, they're ours to do with what we want."

"Again, the operative term being *buy* them," Sarah pointed out. "I thought the idea here is to make money, not spend it."

"Right. But that's the best part," I tried to explain, my mind buzzing with the new plan. "A lot of these stores will buy your old clothes and give you credit to get new ones. I'm sure between all of us we have a whole closet filled with clothes we've grown out of, or don't like anymore, right?"

My friends nodded, considering.

"So we gather everything up," I continued, now on a roll. "We bring it in and sell it. We use the credit to buy four wedding dresses. Then we dye the wedding dresses, maybe add some bling, and voilà! We are perfect princesses."

"You know," Madison said, nodding thoughtfully, "that's not a bad idea."

"I'd much rather be a princess bride than a moth maiden," agreed Kalani.

Sarah scowled. Oh dear.

"You guys go ahead," she said. "I'm going to use one of these."

"Are you sure, Sarah?" I asked, feeling bad. "I mean, don't get us wrong—it was really nice of your mee-maw to offer them. And they're really very beautiful. But they're also kind of old and—"

"What's old can be new again," she declared stubbornly. She grabbed one of the dresses and started pulling it over her head. We watched, giving each other looks, as she struggled to stuff her arms in the narrow sleeves. "I just have to—argh!"

"Do you need some help?"

"I'm fine!"

"You don't look fine."

"It's just a little . . . tight and . . ."

Sarah struggled, attempting to push her head through the small neck hole in the dress, while her arms seemed to get stuck halfway through the sleeves. As she wiggled and contorted her body, it looked as if she was doing some kind of weird dance around the attic.

"There's your real ghost," Madison whispered to Kalani. "The headless corpse bride!"

I glanced over at the spot where the plywood ended and winced as Sarah danced dangerously close to it. "Be careful!" I cried.

But Sarah, still caught in the dress, couldn't see what she needed to be careful about, and as her foot caught under a beam, she went sprawling, hitting the floor hard. A loud ripping sound echoed through the attic. The dress split at the seams. And finally Sarah's head poked through.

"Are you okay?" I asked worriedly.

She gave us a desperate look. Her butt was wedged between two beams, and her feet were sticking up in the air. "Um . . . no?"

We all jumped up and helped her to her feet. Then we attempted to get her out of the dress. Unfortunately, it was stuck fast. Which might have been okay if the zipper in the back hadn't been rusted through. But as it was, the dress clearly wasn't coming back off—at least in one piece.

Sarah gave the chest a regretful look. "Sorry, Mee-Maw," she muttered. Then she looked up at us. "Okay," she said. "On the count of three. One, two . . ."

We each grabbed a piece of the dress, and on three we pulled—tearing it off her body in large strips. Thankfully, the seams gave way easily, and soon Sarah was free . . . with the princess dress nothing more than a pile of shredded fabric on the attic floor.

Not even fit for a ghost.

Sarah shook her head, looking down at what had once been the dress. Then she let out a long sigh before looking back up at us.

"So," she said brightly. "Thrift store, you say?"

7

IT WAS AMAZING WHAT ONE COULD FIND IN ONE'S CLOSET IF
one really dug deep to look. I found jeans I hadn't worn
since I was ten, rolled up in a ball in the back. T-shirts
from every sporting event I'd ever attended with my
dad. Then there was the pile o' itchy sweaters my aunt
was so fond of gifting me every Christmas—with the
price tags still attached. By the time I was finished, I had
quite the haul to bring to the thrift store. And, bonus,
lots of newfound room in my closet for back-to-school
shopping next year.

Kalani talked her brother into taking us down to the
thrift store in their parents' beat-up SUV, and he waited
outside, playing on his phone, while we dragged our

bags into the store and placed them on the counter. The salesclerk popped her gum loudly as she looked over each and every article of clothing individually, judging it on its merits, style, and overall shape. Then, after banging out some pretty crazy calculations even math ninja Madison didn't understand, she handed us a credit slip for a hundred dollars, most of which came from Madison's designer duds. But Madison insisted we just pool the money and buy as much as we could.

"Trust me, I'm just glad to get those hideous things out of my closet," she declared. "Now when my mom says, 'Don't you have anything else to wear?' I can truthfully tell her no." She grinned.

And so, credit in hand, we wandered toward the back of the store, where the wedding gowns were located, and started rummaging through the racks. Kalani scored first—with a bridesmaid's dress that was already a deep purple color and wouldn't have to be dyed. Madison found her dress next—a rather plain, short wedding dress that she insisted she could use as a pirate princess outfit. Sarah appeared a moment later, grinning from ear to ear as she produced some frilly white lacy thing that looked suspiciously like one of her mee-maw's costumes, though thankfully in much better shape.

Unfortunately, I wasn't having as much luck as my friends. Every dress I looked at seemed to be either the wrong size or the wrong look. But I kept searching, determined not to settle for something less than perfection. This was my idea, after all—and I needed to look good. And while I didn't know *exactly* what the perfect princess dress looked like, I was confident I'd know it when I saw it.

And then, lo and behold, I did. Tucked away in a dark corner, separated from the rest of the dresses, as it if had been hiding there so no one could find it except me: a pure white replica of Belle's gown from *Beauty and the Beast*. I drew in a breath, looking it over, my heart pounding in my chest as I searched for any holes or imperfections—there had to be something, right?

But it was perfect. Absolutely perfect. And exactly my size, too. A little yellow dye and it was sure to look epic.

"This is it!" I cried, yanking it from the hanger and holding it up to show my friends. I twirled around and the dress swirled in response, almost causing me to lose my balance. Okay, fine, it was a bit . . . *heavier* than I'd imagined it to be, but once I was wearing it, it should be no big deal.

"Wow," Kalani said. "That's, like, literally the biggest dress in the universe."

"Are you going to be able to babysit in that?" asked Sarah a little doubtfully. "It's so . . . poufy."

"It's so *princessy*!" I corrected, trying not to be offended. Obviously, they were just jealous 'cause their dresses weren't half as amazing as this one. I glanced at the price tag. "Ooh. It's on sale, too! Seventy-five percent off!"

"Can't imagine *why*," muttered Madison. I ignored her. What did she know about princess dresses anyway?

"Okay, let's go buy these things and—"

Suddenly my phone rang. I pushed the dress at Kalani, who almost fell over backward from the sudden weight. As Madison tried to help her wrestle the gown into submission. I reached into my pocket to grab my phone. I squinted down at the caller ID, not sure who it was.

"Hello?" I said, bringing the phone to my ear.

"Hi. Is this the princess babysitter company?" asked a female voice on the other end of the line.

Now it was my turn to almost fall over backward. I looked up at my friends, giving them an excited grin. Our flyers had worked! We had our first customer!

"Um, yes. Sorry. This is Princesses and Pirates, Incorporated. How may I help you?"

There was a pause on the other end of the line. Then: "Okay. Great. My daughter Bella is four years old, and she needs a babysitter Monday at four p.m. Her big sister will be home upstairs doing her homework, so we just need someone to entertain her for a few hours. I was going to use my regular babysitter, but my neighbor gave me your flyer and said you came highly recommended. And Bella loves anything to do with princesses. So I figured I'd give you a try."

It was all I could do not to break out into a Snoopy dance right then and there. I gave my friends a thumbs-up and another crazy grin.

"Yes. Thank you. We appreciate you calling us, and we can totally help you with this. We'll send a princess over at four p.m. on Monday. Thank you. You won't regret your choice. Your daughter is going to love her."

"Wonderful." The mother sounded relieved. "Okay. I'll see you next week."

I took down her address, which thankfully was walking distance from my house, then hung up the phone. Kalani, Sarah, and Madison stared at me with cautiously excited faces. For a moment I stood stock-still, enjoying keeping them in suspense. Then I charged toward them and threw myself into a huge forced group hug.

"Our first job!" I cried. "We got our first job!"

We danced around the thrift shop, cheering, ignoring the annoyed looks of the other customers. Then we gathered up all our dresses and dragged them to the sales counter. (Well, I had to drag mine, anyway—somehow everyone else's dresses seemed suspiciously light.) After paying with our credit, we danced out of the store and to Kalani's brother's waiting SUV.

This was really happening. As of next week we'd be making real money.

We'd be on our way to Comicpalooza. We'd be seeing Collin Prince.

I really needed to get going on that story. . . .

8

"AND NOW, LADIES AND GENTLEMEN, READY OR NOT, I GIVE you . . . Princess Awesome!"

I threw open the bathroom door, pasting a smile on my face, ready to show off my extreme princess makeover to my three friends, who were waiting with bated breath (and possibly a bit of boredom) in the comfort of my bedroom. Sure, it had taken me a little longer than I'd planned to princess up—(okay, a lot longer; who knew this dress had so many buttons and ties?)—but I was hoping the big reveal would make it worth the wait.

It was hard to believe—after a week of planning—that today was finally here. Princesses and Pirates, Incorporated's first official gig: a babysitting job for the

Mitchells' four-year-old daughter, Bella. After some discussion it had been decided that I should take the assignment, seeing as the company was my idea and all, and at this point I was both super excited . . . and scared half to death.

Drawing in a breath (a small one, thanks to the dress's waistline seriously restricting my lung capacity), I readied to make my grand entrance and wow my friends. I grinned as I imagined the looks on their faces as I stepped into the room. The oohs and aahs and cheers that would surely erupt as I paraded around, giving a regal pageant wave. It was going to be epic.

Well, it would be, that was, if I could get the dress's stupid hoop skirt through the bathroom door. I guess I hadn't realized, when I'd brought it in here all folded up, just how wide the thing actually was. But now, I realized belatedly as I attempted a second time to push through the door, I kinda didn't fit.

"Come on, Hailey!" I heard Sarah call from the bedroom. "We want to see!"

"I'll be right there!" I cried with false cheerfulness, trying to wedge my skirt into the doorway. "Just, uh, stay on the bed. Don't move!"

I bit my lower lip, my gaze traveling around the bathroom. Surely this was just a simple matter of physics, right? I mean, real-life people used to wear these things all the time—and they only had tiny outhouses to pee in. There had to be a way to make this work without taking off the hoop skirt and putting it back on outside the bathroom. It had already taken me so long to get dressed in the first place, I was pretty sure my friends would mutiny if I told them ten more minutes. Not to mention I'd be late for the gig.

As I twisted and turned, my underarms prickled with the first signs of sweat, despite the fact that I'd doused myself with deodorant before donning this dress. My body, go figure, did not seem super psyched—or all that forgiving—about being encased in heavy fabric on this eighty degree day. Thank goodness the makeup Sarah had acquired from our school's theater department was waterproof. Otherwise I was pretty sure we'd be forced to change our company name from Princesses and Pirates to Deranged Clowns 'R' Us after the first day on the job.

"Is everything okay, Hailey?"

"It's fine," I ground out through gritted teeth. "Just. Stay. On. The. Bed."

Getting an idea, I backed up. I charged toward the door, hoping the combination of speed and force would push me through.

The good news? It did.

The bad? I couldn't stop once I got through, and I ended up slamming into the opposite wall, then falling into a heap on the floor, taking out the family cat in the process. Bowie let out a loud yowl of protest as he struggled to get out from under my skirts, scratching and clawing at my legs in his panic to get free.

"Ow! Stop it! Bowie! Just calm down and—"

"Hailey?"

"I'm good!"

I was so not good.

"Bowie, get out of there!" I hissed, trying to reach down and grab him from under my skirt. After some searching—this thing had a lot of layers!—finally my fingers connected with fur and I yanked him free, pulling him out from under me and back onto solid ground. He gave me an affronted look, then padded off in the direction of the kitchen, leaving me a sweaty, bedraggled, leg-scratched-up mess.

But there was no way I was risking the bathroom

again. And so, sucking in a (small) breath, I brushed myself off best I could, then headed into the bedroom. I was so exhausted and frazzled at this point, I didn't bother with any parade theatrics—just plopped down on the bed and sighed.

My friends surrounded me.

"What happened?" Sarah cried.

"Are you okay?"

"Princess problems," I muttered. "Who knew?"

"Well, you look amazing," Sarah assured me, reaching over and smoothing out my hair. "Totally ah-MAZ-ing."

"Like a real princess," Madison affirmed, pulling down the hem on my dress and checking out the seams.

"This kid is literally going to die when she sees you," added Kalani as she patted my sweaty face with a huge powder puff.

I stifled a sneeze as powder went up my nose. "I would prefer all kids stay alive on my watch, thank you very much. After all, dead kids would be bad for repeat business."

Kalani snorted. "Well, then figuratively," she amended. "She is *figuratively* going to *die* from all your awesomeness."

"I hope so," I muttered, rising to my feet and glancing in the mirror. My friends had done their best, and I once again looked like my pre–bathroom jailbreak self. A beautiful, sparkling princess without a care in the world.

At least on the outside.

"What's wrong?" Madison demanded. "You're pale as a ghost. You're not nervous, are you?"

"'Cause there's seriously no reason to be nervous," Kalani pointed out. "You're a pro. You practically have your PhD in princess at this point."

"Seriously. You've practiced like a gazillion hours," Sarah reminded me. "You know your stuff."

"I practiced on you guys," I protested. "This is a real-life four-year-old. What if she thinks my magic show stinks?" In preparation for the job, I'd watched all the Collin Prince magic videos so I'd have a few tricks up my sleeve—literally—if things started going downhill. But what if she saw right through them?

"She's four, Hailey. She's not expecting Houdini."

"What if she doesn't believe I'm a real princess?"

"Just smile and tell her the Easter Bunny will vouch for you."

"What if she doesn't listen to what I tell her to do?"

"Threaten to put an evil spell on her!" Kalani chirped, a little too eagerly. "That ought to scare her into submission." She paused, catching our looks. "Or maybe bribe her with chocolate?"

I sighed. "What if—"

"Okay, stop right there, Princess Awesome," Madison interjected. She grabbed my cheeks in her hands and forced me to face her. "You've got this, okay? You're going to be fine. In fact, you're going to wow the doo-doo out of this little girl. And then change her diaper like a boss!"

Everyone burst out laughing. Everyone except me, that was. I was too busy trying to recall whether four-year-olds were commonly potty trained. After all, I didn't exactly relish the idea of diaper duty in this dress.

Was it too late to call this whole thing off?

"Face it, Hails," Madison said. "You're going to rock her world. And her mother will be so impressed by your awesomesauce that she'll go around the neighborhood door to door, telling all her mommy friends that they need to hire us too. I'm telling you, we're going to have more babysitting gigs than we know what to do with."

"*And* more money," Sarah said dreamily. "Though I

know *exactly* what we're going to do with that." She lay back on the bed, stared up at my Collin Prince poster, and sighed happily.

"It will literally be a dream come true," Kalani declared as she joined Sarah's side. "And I mean it this time," she added as we all looked at her. "I have dreams. Actual literal, amazing Collin Prince dreams. And it's going to be just as amazing in real life."

I had to agree. Getting to Comicpalooza would be a dream come true. And if I could pull this off, it would be our reality.

As I turned to meet Collin's dreamy brown eyes with my own, my YouTube idol seemed to smile back at me, reminding me that any pain and suffering and stress I was enduring now would be well worth it in the end.

You can do this, he seemed to say.

And who was I to doubt the great and powerful Collin Prince?

9

TEN MINUTES LATER i WAS AT THE MiTCHELLS' FRONT DOOR.
My friends had wanted to come with me—or at least spy
from the corner—but I'd forced them to stay behind. I
was nervous enough, I'd told them, without an audience
in tow. But now that I was here, standing in front of the
massive oak door, I kind of wished I had my squad.

You can do this, I told myself. *It's just like any other
babysitting job.*

Not that I'd ever had any other babysitting jobs. Or
any jobs, for that matter. Well, besides that time Mrs.
Rathburger went to Florida and I walked her dog. That
was sort of like babysitting, right? She did call the little
guy her fur-baby....

Sucking in a breath, I reached over and pressed the doorbell and waited.

And waited. (And sweated.) And waited. (And sweated some more. April in Texas was so not Princess weather.)

Finally, after I started wondering whether the doorbell might be broken and if maybe I should knock instead, I saw a flash of something behind the window. A moment later the doorknob turned and the door swung open.

"Hello!" I cried cheerfully. "I'm Princess Awesome and—"

"Oh! You're here. Already." The woman at the door—Mrs. Mitchell, I presumed—glanced at her watch with a disapproving eye. She was wearing a bathrobe, and her hair was still soaking wet. My smile faltered a bit.

"You said four, right?" I asked, a little concerned. I hadn't gotten the time wrong, had I? I'd written it down right after our phone conversation at the thrift store and had checked it about ten times since then, just to be sure.

"Oh. Yes. Four. Sorry," she said, giving me a flustered smile. "Where does the time go?" She bit her lower lip. "Sorry, sweetie, come on in. I'm not quite ready, as you can see. But I'm glad you're here. Bella is going to be so surprised."

She put an arm around me and ushered me into the hallway. The blast of air conditioning hit my flushed skin, and I let out a sigh of relief.

"No problem," I told her. "If you want, I can start entertaining her now—while you get ready."

"Oh no. That's okay. I want to be there to see the look on her face. Maybe get some pictures," Mrs. Mitchell explained. She led me down the hall, then reached out to open a door at the other end. A closet door, I realized, a little uneasily. A coat-closet door. And I clearly wasn't wearing a coat.

She looked at me expectantly.

"Um," I said, "I don't understand?"

"I want it to be a *surprise*," she explained, emphasizing the word "surprise" as if she wasn't sure I understood the definition. "You know. Like jumping out of a cake. But a closet instead." She beamed at me. "Bella will love it!"

I stared at her. "So you want me to just . . . wait in the closet?" Oh man. Wasn't this how horror movies started?

"Yes!" She clapped her hands together. "And when she opens the door, I want you to jump out and yell,

'Princess surprise!'" She grinned. "This will be so much fun."

I wasn't so sure about that, but I didn't argue, not wanting to disappoint our very first client during our very first job. After all, we needed her to tell all the other moms in the neighborhood how cool we were and how they needed to hire a princess of their very own. So I obediently shuffled into the closet, best I could, trying to pull in my dress so I could fit.

"Great!" Mrs. Mitchell cried. "See you soon!"

And with that, she shut the door. Leaving me in total blackness.

"Um, you forgot the light?" I called out. But there was no answer, only the sound of footsteps clonking up the stairs above me. A moment later I heard a hair dryer switch on.

O-kay, then. Guess I needed to make myself comfortable.

After adjusting my dress best I could, I practiced muttering 'Princess surprise!' a few times under my breath, trying to get the right tone. Then I tried to think about Comicpalooza and how amazing it was going to be to see Collin Prince and enter the writing competition. *Then* I started wondering just how much oxygen was actually in a small closet like this one and how long it would take to run out. Hypothetically speaking, would one asphyxiate first or die of heatstroke? And which would be the worse way to go?

My heart started beating faster in my chest, the walls of the closet seeming to close in on me like the trash compactor in the first *Star Wars* movie. This was not cool. So not cool. Maybe I should forget this whole thing and—

Suddenly I heard footsteps on the stairs and I let out a breath of relief. Finally. A moment later the door flung open.

"Princess surprise!" I cried, blinking my eyes to adjust to the sudden light.

The teenage girl on the other side of the door screamed. I screamed.

"MOM! THERE'S A PERSON IN THE CLOSET!"

"I know, Trina. Just leave her there for now!" Mrs. Mitchell called down. "I'm not quite ready for her yet."

I gave Trina a pleading look, my heart now pretty much ready to crack a rib it was beating so hard. "I can just wait outside, maybe?" I squeaked. "You know, ring the bell and do the surprise that way?"

Trina shut the door in my face.

I sighed, resigning myself to my fate. *Just a few more minutes*, I told myself. And then the mother would leave and it would just be the kid and me, playing out in the open air.

I felt a twinge in my back from crouching down so long and tried to readjust myself to get more comfortable. It was then that I realized my dress had somehow gotten stuck on the vacuum cleaner in the back of the closet. I reached down and tried to pull it free, but it was stuck fast.

Great. Drawing in a breath, I yanked as hard as I could, somehow managing to knock a fur coat off its hanger in the process. As it dropped down over my head, effectively blinding me, I flailed, tripping over some other unidentified object before crashing into the closet door. Which, unfortunately, it turned out Trina had not shut all the way. As I plummeted onto the hard tile hallway floor, coat still over my head, I heard a terrified scream.

"Monster! *MONSTER!*"

Oh no. I pulled the coat off my head, my eyes falling on a little girl, standing in front of me in a Cinderella dress, a look of abject horror on her toddler face.

"Um, princess surprise?" I tried.

She burst into tears. "Mommy! MOMMMMEEEE!"

"Oh, for goodness sakes!" her mother growled, storming downstairs. "Bella, sweetie, this is not a monster. This is a princess. Princess . . ." She looked at me for help.

Thankfully, I had practiced this part. "Princess Awesome," I declared. "From the faraway kingdom of Awesomeville."

From the corner of my eye I could see Trina roll her eyes. I had to admit, it sounded a lot cooler from the comfort of my bedroom.

"Right," Mrs. Mitchell said. "Bella, this is Princess Awesome. Isn't she pretty? And, uh . . ." She sighed. "Awesome?"

Bella ducked behind her legs. Clearly, she was reserving judgment.

"So wait, *this* is the babysitter you got to watch the turd?" Trina demanded, giving me a critical once-over. "What, is she nine?"

I frowned. "I'm thirteen," I told her. "And I'm very experienced in—"

"Trina, it's going to be fine. You'll be right upstairs if she needs you."

The look on Trina's face told me I'd better not need her. Under any circumstances.

The doorbell rang. Mrs. Mitchell made a move to open it. Bella clung to her leg like one of those koala-bear clips.

"Don't go, Mommy! Please don't go!"

Her mother attempted to pry her off her leg while reaching for the door. "Sweetie, Mommy's got a very important work thing that she has to do, so I need you to be a good girl while I go and—"

"PARTEEE!" cried the woman behind the door. She was wearing a Hawaiian shirt and a bright purple lei.

Mrs. Mitchell turned red. Trina scowled.

"Just so you know, I have a ton of homework," she told her mother. "I am not going to just take over if this chick can't handle the turd."

"MOMMY! DON'T GO, MOMMY!"

"You told me I had the afternoon off. And I am going to take the afternoon off. I am not babysitting under any circumstances."

"PLEEEEASE, MOMMY, DON'T LEAVE!"

Mrs. Mitchell closed her eyes. "Maybe I should just forget this. . . ."

"No!" I cried, practically tripping over my dress in my haste to get to the door. I could not lose this gig. Not now. "You go. Have fun. Or work hard—whatever. We'll be fine, I promise."

I reached into my bag and pulled out my magic wand, a light-up *Frozen* thing I'd found at the thrift store the day we got our dresses. When I pressed the button, Elsa started singing and dancing inside a snow globe.

Bella froze. She turned around, her big brown eyes widening as she stared at the magical wand. I waved it in the air a little, then took a step backward. For a moment she just stood there. Then she released her mother's leg. Took a step forward.

"What's that?" she asked, obviously curious despite her best efforts.

"It's my magic wand," I told her. "I can do all sorts of real magic with it."

From the stairs I could hear Trina's snort. I ignored her. I had Bella's attention, and I wasn't about to lose it.

"Real magic?" Bella repeated. "I want to see some real magic!"

"Well, I can only do real magic without grown-ups

around," I explained. "Otherwise it won't work."

Bella's eyes were wide as saucers now. She turned to her mother. "Go away!" she cried. "I want to see the magic."

I hid a grin. Who was awesome now?

10

MRS. MITCHELL SHOT ME A RELIEVED LOOK. "THEIR FATHER will be home from work in three hours," she told me. "I've left Bella's dinner in the fridge, and she can have some ice cream if she eats all of it."

"Okay," I said. "Don't worry, we'll be fine."

"Come *on*, Darlene!" Her friend grabbed her arm. "We don't want to miss the appetizers!" She glanced over at Trina and me. "Uh, I mean the . . . affidavits? You know . . . for important work purposes?"

Trina stomped back up the stairs. Mrs. Mitchell sighed. She turned to me. "You sure you got this?" she asked.

"Absolutely," I declared. "We're going to have a blast. Aren't we, Bella?"

"A blast!" she confirmed. "Bye, Mommy!" She turned to me. "Let's go do the magic."

Now that's how it's done! I mentally cheered to myself as Bella and I headed for the kitchen, alone at last. Sure, I'd gotten off to a rough start, but now that it was just Bella and me? Everything was going to be fine.

I pulled out my little magic kit, setting out the pieces on the table. Bella watched, her eyes wide and excited. "Do the magic!" she cried. "I want to see the magic."

"Be patient, little princess," I teased. "Good things come to those who wait!"

She beamed, folding her hands in her lap, the picture of a good girl. I grinned. See? This wasn't so hard! Once you got past the costuming and the mom and the crazy closet thing I still couldn't believe she'd subjected me to, it was just plain old babysitting. I could do it with my eyes closed.

My friends were right. We were going to rock this business. We were going to make money hand over foot. We were going to go to Comicpalooza and—

Ding-dong.

"Someone's at the door!" Bella announced cheerfully, sliding off her seat and running toward the entrance.

"Um, maybe we shouldn't . . . um . . ." I ran after her. "We're not supposed to open the door to strangers and—"

Bella yanked the door open. On the other side stood a bored-looking girl about Ginny's age. By her side was a little boy, probably around Bella's age, wearing a *Ninja Turtles* T-shirt. The girl snapped her gum, gave me a skeptical once-over, and then snorted.

"Um, can I help you?" I asked a little doubtfully.

"Oh, look, Tommy!" she cried in the fakest cheery voice ever. "There's a real princess here! Isn't that so cool? I bet she'll want to play with you!"

Tommy gave me a look. Like I was chewed gum he'd found on the bottom of his shoe. "I don't like princesses," he said. "I like ninjas."

"Yeah, well, she's, like, a ninja princess," the girl assured him, shoving him in my direction. I had to take a step back to stop him from stepping on my dress. "I'll be upstairs."

Wait . . . what?

But she was already gone. And the doorbell was ringing again.

In fact, it rang two more times, in quick succession.

With two more teen girls propelling two more bored children in my direction before heading upstairs.

"Trina!" I yelled after the last one. I wanted to stomp upstairs myself, to figure out what was going on here, but I dared not leave three strange children alone with my actual charge. Or, you know, the house they appeared to have made their life's mission to destroy in three minutes or less.

A moment later Trina poked her head down. "What?" she asked, sounding annoyed. As if I were the one being unreasonable here.

I gestured to the kids. "What is this?"

"Sorry," she said, sounding anything but. "A couple friends of mine were also babysitting, and when the kids heard Bella had a princess over, they all wanted to see for themselves." She shrugged. "I didn't think you'd mind."

"You didn't think I'd mind?" I cried, looking at her incredulously.

Her mouth curved into a smug smile. "Yeah. I mean, just think—free publicity for your services. These kids will all go home and tell their parents they want a princess babysitter too!"

"Yeah. But . . ."

"Anyway, we'll be upstairs. Um, studying. Have fun!"

And with that she turned and trounced back upstairs. A moment later I heard music blasting from the direction of her bedroom. I bit my lower lip, looking over my new charges. One kid I could probably handle. But four?

"You're not a *real* ninja princess," Tommy cried, kicking me in the shin.

"She's not a *real* princess at all," sniffed the middle girl, who'd been introduced as Skyler. She stuck her chin up high. "*I've* been to Disney World three times and I've met *all* the princesses. You are not a real princess."

"She is too!" Bella protested, loyally standing by my side. She put her chubby little hands on her waist. "Mommy said so!"

The oldest of the kids, a girl named Izzy, who had to be at least six, rolled her eyes. "Your mom's a liar. There are no such things as princesses. That's just our neighbor in some stupid dress."

Bella regarded me, looking utterly betrayed. "You're not a real princess?" she whimpered. "I thought you were a real princess. You were going to do the magic!"

I sighed. "Bella . . ."

"Actually . . . she's the secret bad guy!" Tommy butted in. "She's come to kill us all!"

Bella burst into tears. And the other kids looked slightly alarmed.

I sighed. "Now, guys, I really don't think—"

But before I could convince them that, while my royal status could possibly come into question, I was definitely *not* here on a mission to murder them and sincerely wished them the best, even if I didn't want them here, under my care, Tommy turned to the others. He raised his hand, like he was the commanding general of his own army.

"Get her!" he crowed. "Get the bad guy!"

I screamed as the children all charged at once. All four of them threw themselves on top of me. Even if I'd been dressed in street clothes I would have had little chance of escape. But in a fancy dress I was doomed. As I fell to the floor, my foot stepped on the hem of my dress, and a ripping noise rang through the air.

Oh no. No, no, *no*!

"I see London, I see France. I see Princess's

underpants," chanted Skyler happily as I tried to scramble back to my feet.

Worst. Babysitting. Gig. Ever.

As the four kids danced around me, I found myself glancing longingly at the front door. How bad would it be to just run away? The kids wouldn't be alone—Trina and her friends were right upstairs. I could just chalk this whole thing up to a terrible idea and move on with a princess-free life from this point forward.

But then I thought about my friends. How excited they'd been. How disappointed they'd be. If I gave up now, on the first day of the job, we'd never have a second. We'd never make any money. And we'd never get to Comicpalooza.

No. My friends were counting on me. I couldn't let them down. We'd worked too hard to set this up. I wasn't going to allow myself to be thwarted by a bunch of little kids.

I was Princess Awesome, after all. And Princess Awesome didn't need some fairy godmother to come rescue her when things got tough.

Princess Awesome saved herself.

I reached into my bag, pulled out my whistle, put

it to my lips, and blew as loud as I could.

All four kids froze, turning to me. I drew in a breath. Here went nothing.

"Line up!" I cried. "And be quiet! 'Cause this princess party is about to get real."

11

THE KiDS LOOKED ME WiTH SUSPiCiON iN THEiR EYES, BUT thankfully, they shuffled into something that vaguely resembled a line. When Skyler opened her mouth to speak, I shook my head at her.

"My turn," I said. "And listen up. I'm about to tell you a secret."

Skeptical looks from my peanut gallery, but I had their attention still. I'd take what I could get.

I drew in a breath. Here went nothing.

"Tommy, you are correct. I am not a ninja princess. Nor, as Skyler so helpfully pointed out, am I a Disney princess. However, I am also not a bad guy. And I am not here to murder anyone. So you can all relax about that.

But . . . ," I added, a smile creeping across my face, "I do have a secret identity."

I paused for dramatic effect. Now I had their full attention. They were so quiet, in fact, you could have heard a pin drop. (Well, you could have, anyway, had Trina's music not been blasting from upstairs.)

"So who are you, then?" Tommy blurted out at last.

I gave him an ultraserious look. "If I tell you, you have to promise to keep it quiet. No one can know about this. Especially not your parents. It's very important."

They all nodded. Solemn looks all around.

"Okay, then," I said. "I feel like I can trust you. So I will tell you my secret." I was starting to enjoy this game. It was kind of like writing a story, on the fly—making it up as I went along. "I am a pirate princess," I declared. "And I am on the hunt for a very valuable treasure. One that was stolen from my family a long, long time ago. I have recently uncovered a secret map that has led me here to Bella's backyard. I believe the legendary treasure I seek might be out there, somewhere, just waiting to be found."

Izzy opened her mouth to speak. I shot her a warning look.

"Now, I don't usually do this. I actually prefer to

work alone. But this is a big job and I don't have much time. If I'm going to locate the treasure before your dad gets home, Bella, I'm going to need some help." I paused. "Is there anyone here interested in helping me?"

"Do we get to keep the treasure?" Tommy demanded.

I pretended to consider this. "Maybe," I said at last. "If I decide you've done a good job searching. Then I will consider splitting the treasure with you."

"Sweet!" Tommy declared.

Izzy rolled her eyes. "Come on," she said. "We all know there isn't any treasure."

I gave her a look. "And you know this . . . how?"

She frowned. "It's obvious. You're just making it up."

"Okay." I held up my hands. "That's fine. You're more than welcome to go upstairs and find your babysitter and let her know you want to go home. We'll split up your share of treasure amongst ourselves. More for all of us that way anyway."

She frowned, shuffling from foot to foot. I held my gaze, as if daring her to walk away. I could almost see the gears whirring in her head. She knew she shouldn't believe me. But a tiny part of her still clung to that child-hood innocence and wanted to.

"I guess it couldn't hurt to look," she muttered at last.

"Whatever you want to do," I said briskly, then turned to Bella, dropping down to my knees in front of her and taking her hands in mine. "Now as for you, my sweet girl, I have a very special job in mind. Would you be my personal princess assistant during the treasure hunt?"

Bella nodded eagerly. "Yes!" she cried. "I can do that. I'll be the best princess assistant ever!"

I smiled at her. "Excellent." I handed her my bag of magic tricks—just in case I needed them—then turned back to the others. "If everyone's in agreement, I think we should get started."

I rose to my feet and pushed open the back door that led into the yard. Once we were all outside, I started shouting commands to each of the kids, and they spread out, starting their treasure hunt. Tommy and Skyler were soon full-on into the game, whereas Izzy kind of hung back, making a great show of looking bored. I sighed, wondering how long it would take for her to ruin the game for the others. And what I would do for my next act once they mutinied again.

"Wow! This looks *way* better than a boring old babysitter!"

I whirled around at the sound of the voice, only to find none other than Brody himself standing nearby, a teasing smirk on his face. Relief washed over me at seeing a familiar face.

"What are you doing here?" I asked.

"I live next door." He gestured to the house behind him.

"Wow. That's so random."

"Not really." He grinned, looking proud of himself. "Remember that day you gave me the flyers to hand out?" After I nodded, he added, "Well, I might have just happened to swing by my next-door neighbor's house and hand-deliver one right after that chance meeting, along with my personal recommendation, of course."

"So wait—you're the one who got us this job?" I exclaimed, glancing over at the kids, who were already looking as if they were losing motivation. I wasn't sure whether to thank Brody or curse him for this gesture of goodwill.

He grinned. "I just passed out a flyer. But I'm glad it worked out."

"Um. Worked out might be a bit . . . overstating things," I muttered.

"What do you mean?"

I gestured to the kids. "I'm pretty sure I'm only minutes away from a complete mutiny once they discover the hidden treasure is . . . well, not exactly hidden. Or, you know, treasure."

Brody listened as I explained the whole fiasco—being dumped with extra kids, their not believing me to be a princess, my desperate pirate scheme. When I had finished, he nodded thoughtfully.

"I think there's only one answer here," he declared.

"Me running away?"

He laughed. "Look. Can you distract them for a few minutes? I've got an idea."

"What's that?"

"You need pirate treasure, right? What if I went and hid some?"

"You have spare pirate treasure lying around in your living room?"

"Doesn't everyone?"

I laughed. "Not me. If I did, I wouldn't have to be babysitting in the first place."

"Good point." He gave me a grin. "Now. Can you distract them for a few minutes so they won't catch me?"

I nodded. "But be quick—they have the attention spans of angry gnats!"

"Aye, aye, Captain." He gave me a salute, then ran back into his yard and disappeared through his front door. I watched him go, then turned back to the kids.

"Guys!" I cried, beckoning them over. "Circle round. We need to talk."

The kids ran over to me. They didn't look happy. "I haven't found *any* treasure," Tommy complained.

"That's because there isn't any," Izzy sniffed.

Out of the corner of my eye I caught Brody leaving the house again, out the back door this time, tiptoeing across his yard and into Bella's. He was carrying a large sack—presumably the so-called treasure.

Skyler started to turn around. I clapped my hands to get her attention. No matter what I had to do, I couldn't let them see Brody. That would ruin the game altogether.

"There is a good reason you haven't found the treasure," I declared.

"What's that?" demanded Skyler.

"Because the treasure is . . ." I trailed off, my mind racing. I watched Brody slip behind a tree. Disappearing from sight. "INVISIBLE!" I cried.

Three of the four children screwed up their faces. Only Bella looked as if she still held out some belief that this could possibly be true.

"That's the stupidest thing I've ever heard," Izzy muttered.

"How are we supposed to find the treasure if it's invisible?" Skyler demanded.

"I know! I know!" Bella cried. She turned to me, her eyes shining. "You can do the magic, right? You can make it un-invisible?"

I nodded solemnly, as if that were obvious. *Thank you, Bella.* She'd definitely earned an extra scoop of ice cream after this was all over. "Actually, I can. But I'll need all of your help to do it. Are you willing to help me?"

"Yes!" Bella cried.

The others didn't look quite so sure, but to their credit they didn't say no outright. Reaching into my magic bag, while keeping an eye on Brody, who was still traversing the yard, bag in his hand like some pirate Santa Claus, I pulled out my magic snow powder. This was something I'd discovered from watching a Collin Prince *Frozen* parody video a year ago, and it was pretty much my coolest trick. Hopefully it would work under pressure.

"Okay," I said. "Who wants to hold the magic powder?"

They all did, so I poured a little in each kid's hand. Then I reached into my bag again, pulled out my vial of water, and cupped it in my hand so they couldn't see it. A magician was all about misdirection, as I'd learned from Collin, the master magician.

"Okay. Close your eyes," I said. "On the count of three I want you to yell, 'Treasure appear!' Okay?"

"Okay!" they agreed, with varying levels of enthusiasm.

I drew in a breath. Here went nothing. I waited until all their eyes were closed, then counted them down as I got my water ready. "Three, two . . . one!"

"TREASURE APPEAR!"

I dripped water into each of their hands.

"Okay! Open your eyes!"

They did, all four of them shrieking in delight as the tiny drops of magical powder in their hands expanded into entire fistfuls of flaky white snow. I smiled to myself. Score another for Princess Awesome.

"Okay!" I said. "It appears the spell has worked. Now all the treasure should be revealed. Go forth and search again."

I waved my arms in the air, sending them back to the

yard, hoping Brody had had enough time to do his thing. I watched as they spread out again, still excited about the magic powder, which in hindsight I realized could have been a treasure all its own.

"You guys! I found something!" Tommy shrieked a moment later. "Come here!"

Yes! I mentally raised my fist in triumph. *Go, Brody!*

I ran over to see what he had found. He held up what looked like a tennis ball, but painted gold. Perhaps very recently painted gold, in fact, judging from the gold paint now all over Tommy's hand. Thankfully, Tommy didn't seem to notice that.

"Wow, that's amazing, Tommy!" I cried. "Quick, put it in my bag." I held out the bag and he threw it in. "I wonder if there's any more—"

"Look, look!" squealed Izzy, interrupting in a voice filled with excitement. Everyone ran to where she was standing. She held up an old bronze statue of a bucking bronco the size of her arm. "Do you think this is treasure too?" she asked, looking quite pleased with herself.

"Oh, definitely," I agreed, stifling a grin as I took the horse from her and placed it in my bag. These were definitely *interesting* treasures, that was for sure. "Let's keep looking."

Now the kids were truly into the game, running all over the yard looking for more treasure. Over the next ten minutes they acquired a crystal vase, a pewter spoon, a macramé owl pot holder, and a plastic light-up version of Darth Vader's lightsaber. It was the most unusual and yet most awesome treasure trove a pirate could ever hope to have.

From across the yard, Skyler suddenly screamed in delight. "Come here! Come here!" she cried, waving us over.

We joined her under an old oak tree, right on the border of where Brody's yard met Bella's. There, nestled under a bush, was a small wooden chest.

"A real pirate chest!" she announced proudly.

I grinned. Brody deserved more than an extra scoop of ice cream. Maybe even an extra large hot fudge sundae.

"All right," I declared. "This is it. The last treasure. Let's go ahead and open it and then we can all—"

"ARRR!"

A sudden cry echoed through the yard, causing the kids to shriek in alarm. They scrambled behind me,

Tommy clinging to my leg, Izzy and Skyler to my arms—shaking like crazy.

The voice came again, seeming to ring through the air. "ARRRR! Who goes there?"

I stifled a giggle as Brody jumped out from behind the tree, nearly losing his balance as his foot caught on an upturned root. He was dressed in pirate gear from head to toe—a bandana around his head and an eye patch over his left eye. Raising his pirate sword in the air, he winked at me with his non-eye-patched eye and then turned to the kids.

"And what might ye be doing with me treasure?" he demanded, giving my little crew a suspicious once-over.

"Nothing!" Skyler cried, looking petrified. "We were just . . . looking at it!"

"We weren't going to steal it!" Izzy protested. "Really."

Pirate Brody narrowed his eyes. "Then what be in yer pocket, me laddie?" he demanded, pointing at Tommy's pocket. Which, I realized, was glowing bright purple—one of the glow sticks he'd found in the yard. Tommy swallowed hard, fear clear in his eyes, and I did my best not to crack up laughing.

"I was just . . . keeping it safe for you?" he tried.

"A likely story," Brody snarled. "I think you tried to steal it from me. And now you must pay the pirate price." He paused. "Unless there be a champion amongst you who will save the day . . ."

He turned to me, shooting me an encouraging look. I drew in a breath and stepped forward.

"Nay, it is you, Dread Pirate Brody, who has stolen from me. This treasure has been in my family for generations. And now I will finally reclaim it."

"Over my dead body," scoffed Brody.

"If you like." I stepped forward, reaching down to Bella and retrieving my bag of tricks. After rummaging around for a second, I pulled out my Elsa wand. Not exactly a sharp blade, but it would have to do for now. "Prepare to meet your maker!"

I waved the wand. Brody raised his sword, his eyes flashing with mischief. He lunged forward, but I easily parried, knocking him back. We went back and forth like this a few times, with the kids all watching with anxious eyes.

"Use your magic!" Bella cried out from the sidelines. "Princess Awesome! USE YOUR MAGIC!"

I gave Brody a knowing look, then held up my free

hand and whooshed it in his direction. "Stand down, evil pirate!" I cried.

Brody staggered backward, clutching his chest with his hands, as if he really had been hit by a mighty force. I had to admit: The guy made a very good pirate.

"NO!" he screamed—a little overdramatically in my opinion, but the kids were totally eating it up, so who was I to judge? "You are a vile sorceress! How dare you use your magic on me!"

"There's a lot more where that came from," I declared. "And if you do not yield, I will be forced to use it."

Brody whimpered, dropping low before us, bowing in submission. "Please," he warbled. "I'll be a good pirate. You can have your treasure back. Just . . . don't use your magic!"

I glanced over at the kids. "What do you think?" I asked. "Should we let him go?"

Even as I asked, I wondered what I was going to do if they demanded actual blood. But thankfully, this crew was too concerned about their treasures to worry much about true justice being served, and they decided on mercy.

"Very well," I said, giving Brody a stern look. "We

will let you go. As long as you promise to be a good pirate from now on. And never terrorize anyone from this day forward."

"I promise," he said, looking relieved. He staggered to his feet.

"Now go!" I commanded. "And let us never see your face here again!"

And with that, he took off, running into the next yard and disappearing from sight. I watched him go—a small smile playing at my lips. We had managed to pull it off . . . together.

Or almost, at least. I still had to bring this big bad princess party home.

I turned to the kids, a triumphant smile on my face. "It appears evil has been vanquished," I announced. "So how about we round up the rest of the treasure and celebrate our victory—with ice cream?"

12

AFTER THAT, THE KIDS ALL SETTLED IN THE LIVING ROOM, looking over their treasure. I told them they could each keep one piece—or I could buy it all back from them in exchange for an extra scoop of ice cream—a deal they were all happy to accept. They were playing happily when the other babysitters finally emerged from upstairs. They stared at the kids, then at me.

"So, uh, how it'd go?" Skyler's babysitter asked.

"Best. Babysitter. Ever!" Skyler cried. "Do we have to leave?"

"Yes. Your mother will be back any second now. And you know she doesn't want you out of the house."

I raised an eyebrow, an idea coming to me. I walked

over to the babysitter and held out my hand. She looked down at it, then up at me. "What?" she asked in an annoyed voice.

"That'll be ten bucks," I said.

"Excuse me?"

"Oh. I just figured, since I was doing your job all afternoon, I should probably get paid for it."

She wrinkled her nose. "You were so not doing my job. We just happened to come over to visit."

"Oh. Okay. That's fair. If you don't want to pay me, then I can swing by Skyler's house on the way home. I'm sure her mother will hook me up once I explain my services to her."

The babysitter's eyes widened. She reached into her pocket and shoved a crinkled ten in my direction. Bingo.

"Whatever," she muttered. "Come on, Skyler. Let's go." She dragged the girl out of the house. Skyler gave her a nasty look, then ran back to me.

"Thank you!" she cried. "You're the best babysitter ever!"

I gave her a hug. "Tell your mom," I whispered. "And maybe next time she'll hire me instead."

She grinned. "I will."

The babysitter rolled her eyes and grabbed Skyler, shoving her out the door. A moment later the next babysitter came down the stairs. I smiled and held out my hand.

In the end I collected forty extra bucks (with the final ten coming from Trina, who didn't want me to tell her mother), and after dinner Bella and I spent the rest of the time together, playing Candyland. By the time her father came home, the little girl was asleep on the couch, thumb securely locked in her mouth.

He raised an eyebrow. "How did you manage to get the perpetual-motion machine to crash?" he teased.

I smiled. "A princess never tells."

He paid me—double what I had asked for—and I headed out the door, practically dancing. A few hours of work and I'd scored almost a hundred dollars. We were well on our way to Comicpalooza. My friends were going to completely freak.

"Well, well, well. If it isn't the all-powerful party princess herself."

I looked up, surprised to see Brody, watching me from his front porch. He leaped over the railing and headed in my direction. His pirate gear was gone, and he was dressed in jeans and a T-shirt that totally brought out his eyes. Not that I was noticing stuff like that.

"Hey," I said, smiling at him. "I suppose you want your treasure back."

"Aye, lassie. Hand it over before me mother comes home and thinks someone robbed the house." He laughed, taking the bag from me and pulling out the artifacts. "Not bad for last-minute scrounging though, right?"

"Amazing. The gold-painted tennis ball was a particularly special touch. I can't believe no one wanted to bring it home with them."

"Yeah, that one might have gone over better if it had time to dry." He snorted. "I was originally going to do a bunch of those until I realized how messy it would be."

"Hey! Beggars can't be choosers," I assured him with a smile. "And trust me, the kids didn't even notice. They were just excited to find *any* treasure out there in the backyard."

"Find treasure *and* fight a real pirate prince. Not bad for one afternoon."

"Yes. Thanks to you."

He waved me off. "It was an honor and a privilege to serve, m'lady," he quipped. "And just think. You're one step closer."

Now I gave him a puzzled look. What?

"You know," he said. "The writing contest. That's why you're doing this, right? So you can get to Comicpalooza and launch your writing career?"

"Oh. Right." I nodded quickly. Probably too quickly. "Of course. I didn't . . . Yeah. My writing career. One step closer."

"Have you started your story yet?" he asked. "'Cause I'd be happy to read it if you wanted me to. I'm no writer—but my dad always says it helps him to have people read his stuff before he passes it in to his editor. They can catch stuff he can't see." He shrugged. "But . . . I would understand if you wanted to keep it private, too," he amended.

I stared at him, my heart pounding in my chest. He wanted to read my writing? But I barely had any writing. I mean, at least not for the contest. I'd written some pages, but thrown most of them away. Which meant the only thing I *did* have was the fan fiction stuff for my friends about Collin Prince. And I couldn't show him that. That would be way too embarrassing. Especially with his dad being a real author and all. He probably read good stuff all the time.

But . . . he wanted to read my writing! And maybe he'd even show his dad, and his dad could give me pointers. Pointers that might help me actually win this contest. Get the scholarship to the writing camp.

"No, that would be . . . great," I managed to squeak out. "But, uh, I'm still working on it, you know? When I'm done, I'll totally let you read it, though. If the offer still stands."

He nodded solemnly. "It'll still stand," he agreed. "As long as *your* offer still stands to go play PlayStation at your house sometime. I'm pretty much dying of withdrawal at this point."

I grinned. "Well, we certainly can't let *that* happen. After all, if you're dead, who will edit my story?"

"Ouch!" he cried, holding his hands over his chest as if I had wounded him. "Right to the heart."

I giggled. "Don't worry. The offer still stands," I assured him. "In fact, if you want we could go play right now."

13

"SO WHERE'S THE NEXT PART?" SARAH DEMANDED, POUNCING
on me the second I sat down at the lunch table the next
day, nearly upsetting my tray. "Tell me you brought a
new part."

Uh-oh. I bit my lower lip. I knew there was *something* I
forgot to do. After the babysitting gig yesterday and then
having Brody come over to play PlayStation and then
doing my homework, I'd forgotten all about the Collin
Prince chapter I'd promised her.

Okay, fine. I hadn't completely forgotten. It was
just that hanging around Brody had made me want to
work on my *other* story—the one I was going to enter

in the Comicpalooza contest. I needed that story to be especially good, seeing as it would be read and judged by actual editors, versus just my Collin Prince–crazy friends, who would pretty much love garbage so long as Collin Prince was the garbage man. Which meant it was going to take a lot longer to write.

I had planned to wake up early this morning to bang out a quick chapter to bring to school—to get Sarah off my back. But I'd been so exhausted from the babysitting adventure, I'd hit snooze three times on my alarm. And it wasn't until now that I remembered why I'd set it for so early in the first place.

Should I confess about having Brody come over? She'd freak out if I did. After all, I wasn't the type of girl who normally invited real-life boys over to my house. And boy crazy Sarah might decide to make more of it than it actually was. Like a real date. Me having a new boyfriend. (Or *any* boyfriend for that matter.)

And what if she told someone about it and it ended up getting back to Brody? And what if Brody didn't actually like me in that way—and just thought of me as a fellow gamer—a cool friend, nothing more? At that point, I would pretty much have to die of humiliation.

Clearly it was better to keep the whole Brody thing on the down low for now. . . .

I realized Sarah was still waiting for an answer.

"Sorry. I didn't have time to work on it," I told her apologetically. "I had that babysitting job, remember? You're welcome to keep going on your end, though, if you want. I'll catch up wherever you leave off."

She frowned. "Hailey, I've done three chapters in a row now, and you haven't done any," she whined. "I can't write the whole thing myself."

"You mean like *I* was doing before you decided to jump in?" I shot back before I could stop myself.

She looked hurt, and I immediately felt bad. After all, I had been the one to invite her to contribute to the story in the first place. And she'd done a great job, too.

That said, I didn't like the idea that now something I had once done for fun was starting to feel like more homework, complete with unreasonable deadlines.

"Look, I'm sorry," I said. "I know I'm behind. I promise I'll write the next chapter tonight. And I'll upload it right away so you won't have to wait."

"Wait for what?" Madison asked, thankfully showing up with her mountainous tray of food before Sarah could open her mouth to argue further. She plopped down beside me. "'Cause I really don't want to wait to hear how it went yesterday at the Mitchells'. Did they love your dress? Did the little girl think you were a real princess? Did she like your magic show?"

"Wait, wait! I want to hear too!" Kalani cried, rushing to her seat, late as per usual. "Tell us everything!"

I looked around the table at my friends. Their eager faces. "Well," I said. "There were some good things—and some not-so-good things. But mostly good in the end."

They listened without interrupting as I proceeded to give them the play-by-play for the afternoon from beginning to end. When I finished, they were all wide-eyed.

"Seriously?" Kalani cried. "They locked you in a closet?"

"And you had to babysit four kids for the price of one?" Madison added.

"Who was this cute pirate boy again?" demanded Sarah, even though I hadn't even remotely implied he was cute.

I rolled my eyes. "Yes, not exactly, and his name's Brody," I said, answering them all at once. Then I went on to explain my little babysitter blackmail scheme and the fact that Bella's father had given me a 100 percent tip. All of which I would deposit into our Comicpalooza savings account.

"That is awesome," Madison declared. "I cannot believe they thought they could just take advantage of you like that. You totally deserved that extra money."

"Yeah, and now the kids they were babysitting are going to go home and ask for us next time instead!" Kalani crowed. "Those girls, like, literally gave us their customer base."

"Hold on. *I* still want to know more about this Brody guy," Sarah broke in, waving her hands in my direction. The girl could be like a pit bull with a bone when it came to boy talk.

I sighed, knowing there was no way I was going to be allowed to leave the lunchroom until I gave her the scoop on my new friend. And so I went through the story, explaining how I'd first met him while hanging up the flyers and how he'd gone and recommended us to the Mitchells, giving us our first job. I ended by telling them how he'd overheard my desperate pirate talk from next door and had decided to come to my aid.

"Wow," said Madison when I had finished. "That's awesome."

"He's like your knight in shining armor," declared Kalani.

"This would be great for the next chapter of our story!" Sarah exclaimed. "A brave, valiant hero—saving his favorite damsel in distress! But, of course," she added, perhaps unnecessarily, "in this case the hero would be Collin Prince. And I'd be the one in distress." She mock-swooned, and Madison rolled her eyes.

"For the record, I wasn't *that* distressed," I protested. But then—because who was I kidding?—I allowed myself a small dreamy smile. "Though I have to admit, he did have pretty great timing. And the whole treasure thing was a brilliant idea. The kids totally freaked."

Everyone nodded in agreement. "Too bad you can't use him every time," Madison remarked. "Sounds like the two of you made a good team."

I nodded slowly. "You know, maybe we should consider something like that. . . ."

"Having cute boys rescue us?" Sarah asked eagerly. "Absolutely. Where do I sign up?"

I laughed. "I meant the teamwork thing," I clarified.

"After all, if I've learned anything from this whole adventure, it's that it's tough to babysit solo. Especially when wearing a fancy dress." I snorted, remembering. "But if there were two of us at every job, we'd always have each other as backup if things started going bad. Or even if they didn't, it would give us a lot more opportunities to put on a show like Brody and I did. Like, we're kind of boring by ourselves," I said. "But together . . . we could be amazing."

"Yeah. But who's going to pay for two babysitters?" asked Madison.

"No one," I assured her. "We'll still charge the same. It'll be like another bonus of hiring us over the others in the neighborhood. Two babysitters for the price of one."

"Which means only half the money," Kalani protested.

"At first, maybe. But we'll be able to do a better job. And more moms will want to hire us. Which will lead to more money in the end." I shrugged. "I don't know. It'd probably be a lot more fun, too. We did start this company together, after all."

"Well, I think it's a great idea," Sarah declared. "I was kind of dreading doing it by myself anyway, to be honest. I've never really been around a lot of kids. . . ." She paused, then added, "Maybe you could ask Brody to join us from time to time too. I mean, not officially or anything. My parents would flip out if they knew I was alone in some house with a boy. But he could be, like, behind the scenes. Planting treasure, making maps, staging fight scenes—whatever."

"I don't know," I hedged. "He did ask if he could join. I just thought you guys wouldn't want to share the profits a fifth way."

Madison waved me off. "Like you said, the better we perform, the more profit we'll get. And if this Brody guy can help, well, then let's get him on board."

"If you're sure," I said, giving in. Because, of course I *wanted* Brody to join us. I just didn't want them to think I was choosing a boy over my besties. But if it was their idea, who was I to complain?

It was then that I remembered the whole Comic-palooza thing. Brody thought I was going for the writing contest. If my friends started talking about Collin Prince in front of him . . .

I swallowed hard. "Okay, I'll ask him," I said. "On one condition."

"What's that?"

"When he's around, we don't talk about Collin Prince."

My friends exchanged looks. "Why not?" Kalani demanded.

I could feel my face flush. "It's just . . . I don't know . . ."

"I do!" Sarah crowed. She turned to Madison and Kalani, giving them a conspiratorial look. "She *likes* Brody."

Oh man. Now I was positive I was bright purple. "That's not why!" I protested.

My friends giggled. "Mm-hm," Madison said. "Sure it isn't."

"He's just a friend!"

"For now," Kalani teased. "But once you start babysitting with him . . ."

"Seriously. One more word and I will strangle all of you at once."

Sarah laughed. "Don't worry!" she cooed. "We won't say a word about Collin to Brody." She winked at me. "As long as I get that next chapter, that is . . ."

14

BRODY, OF COURSE, WAS HAPPY TO HAVE THE OPPORTUNITY
to join us, and we spent the next day's lunch period
creating scripts to go along with our potential new gigs.
Pirates and princesses were definitely more fun when
mixed together, and we wrote some scenarios where
the princesses were the good guys and some where they
were evil—and where the pirates were forced to defend
the kids against the cruel monarchy.

There was only one thing that Madison insisted be in
every script. That the princesses could never be wimpy.
They could never sit around, waiting in a tower. Or fall
asleep and need some random dude with a crown to
wake them up with a "true-love kiss."

We princesses saved ourselves, y'all.

When I retrieved my phone from my locker that afternoon, I found three messages waiting for me, from parents around the neighborhood who had heard about my adventures with Bella. One was actually Izzy's mother, who told me her "too cool for school" six-year-old who normally hated babysitters had come home gushing about pirate adventures—and could I come by on Saturday for a couple of hours while she ran errands?

Score! I grinned to myself. Izzy's regular babysitter was going to be so mad when she realized she'd been replaced. But hey—that was her fault, right? After all, Izzy wouldn't even know my awesome babysitting skills existed if her babysitter hadn't dumped her on me in the first place.

Thursday night I finally had a chance to sit down at my computer and created a new Google calendar and shared it with my friends. Then I marked the three jobs and, after some thought, paired everyone up. I would take Izzy on Saturday—with a little help from Brody behind the scenes. Madison and Kalani could take the Jacksons' three-year-old twin girls Wednesday after school. Which left the third job—a Friday night assignment for a five-year-old boy who was obsessed with Captain Hook. That had Madison's name written all over it, and I could be the assist.

When I finished, I leaned back in my seat, looking over the calendar. I was no math ninja like Madison, but I could practically see the money adding up on the screen all the same. Three hours, four hours, two hours. Thirty, seventy, ninety dollars. And that was all in one week. If we kept this schedule up, we'd have no problem getting the money raised in time for Comicpalooza.

Feeling pretty good about things, I opened up Microsoft Word and pulled up my Collin Prince story. I'd managed to write half a chapter over the weekend, but Sarah had burned through that in like three seconds this morning and had demanded the rest—stat. Feeling bad that I'd been such a lazy writer, I'd decided to finish up the chapter for her before getting back to my homework.

Okay, fine, *starting* my homework. Turned out, making the calendar had taken a little longer than I'd thought. Now it was almost eight o'clock and I hadn't even cracked a book. But, I told myself, this was just a one-time thing, and now that the calendar was made, it would just need to be updated. So no big deal. Unlike the never-ending flow of homework my teachers seemed to feel the need to dish out every night. Bleh.

I swear, sometimes homework felt like a really bad video game—the kind with endless repeating quests. You worked your butt off to unlock the next level, defeat the bad boss, turn that quest in, and then—bam! You got another one, just like it. Sure, you got "experience points" (or, in this case, "grades"), but there had to be a better way, right?

That was one reason I liked writing so much. Stories had a beginning, middle, and end. No matter where you were in the process, you knew where you stood. How far you had to go. And when you did finish, you got this total sense of accomplishment, writing "the end."

Of course, at the moment I was very far from the end.

I shook my head, trying to focus. I typed a sentence. I stared at the screen. Then I typed another sentence. And stared at the screen again. Then I read over the two sentences and deleted the first—which wasn't very good. Ugh.

Feeling suddenly depressed, I scrolled up to the top of the document. To the very first chapter I'd written at the beginning of the school year. At the time I'd been so excited to share this story with my friends. But now, reading it over, it sounded so stupid. How did I ever think this was any good? What would Brody think if he read this? His dad was a real author, after all.

Sighing, I switched over to my other story. The one I'd started working on for the competition. I read it over—it wasn't long—and when I got to the end, I tried typing a new sentence.

But the words refused to come. And I found myself staring at a blank page again. One thing about the Collin Prince story—I had no problem coming up with what happened next. After all, my friends were very clear as to how they wanted things to go.

But for this story . . . I needed to do better. Serious fiction, after all, was supposed to say something important. That was what my English teacher always said, anyway. That there was always a serious message, written between the lines.

All I saw between *my* lines, however, was white space.

Endless, nonspeaking, white space.

I slumped in my chair, scrubbing my face with my hands. It didn't help that I was so tired. Which wasn't good. I had to work on the Collin Prince story or

Sarah would kill me. And I had to keep working on the Comicpalooza story or I'd have nothing to show Brody. And then, of course, there was my homework. But I didn't even want to think about that yet.

Suddenly there was a knock on my door. My stepmother poked her head in.

"How's the homework going?" she asked.

"Um, great!" I lied, quickly closing my browser window. "Just about done, actually."

"Good girl," she said. Then she held out her phone. "Your father wanted to FaceTime, but he didn't want to disturb you if you were in the middle of something."

I leaped from my seat, eager for the distraction. "Thanks!" I said, grabbing the phone from her, then giving her a meaningful look. Thankfully, she got the hint and exited the room, closing the door behind her. Once she was gone, I climbed onto my bed and pulled my knees up to my chest, resting the phone on top of them.

"Hey, Dad," I said, smiling into the camera.

He smiled back at me. "Hey, princess," he said, his voice a little crackly. The Wi-Fi in his apartment in China was always a bit sketchy, to say the least. "How's everything going over there?"

I stole a glance over at my computer and the two unfinished stories mocking me next to an unopened history book.

"Great!" I chirped. "Really great!"

My dad gave me a suspicious look. I knew it was tough for him to be stationed over in China for months on end, leaving me to live with my stepfamily. At times I wasn't sure what made him feel guiltier, leaving me stuck with my stepmom or leaving my stepmom stuck with me.

"And you've been behaving yourself? Not giving your stepmother any more grief about that comic book convention?"

"No, Dad." Ugh. I still couldn't believe she went and told him about that.

"She felt really bad having to say no," he continued, as if I had demanded some explanation. "But you know money is tight right now, right, sweetheart? There's really not a lot of room in the budget for trips this year."

I balled my hands into fists, off-camera so he couldn't see. "I *know*, Dad," I said through clenched teeth. "It's fine. I was disappointed for, like, a second. She *really* didn't need to mention it."

"Honey, she's just worried about you," my father

responded, as I knew he would. Always taking her side, even though I was the one who was blood-related. He gave me a sympathetic look. "My baby girl," he said. "You know I would give you the entire world, wrapped in ribbon, if only I could."

I felt a lump form in my throat, despite my best efforts. It was something he used to say to me when I was little. Dad's life savings were pretty much drained in his attempt to save Mom's life with an experimental treatment that wasn't covered by insurance. (And didn't work in the end.)

"I know, Dad," I said, swallowing down the lump best I could. "And really, it's okay. I swear. My friends and I . . . well, we found a way to make some money on our own. To pay for the trip ourselves."

His face brightened. "That's wonderful, sweetheart." A mischievous smile flashed across his mouth. "I assume whatever it is, it's legal?"

I laughed. "It's babysitting, Dad!" I told him. "Princess babysitting."

"You're babysitting princesses? Well, la-dee-dah!"

"No. We're princess babysitters." I quickly explained the whole idea. When I had finished, he gave a low whistle.

"My little entrepreneur," he said. "You're going to be running the whole world someday, the rate you're going."

"Eh." I waved him off. "Running the world sounds pretty stressful. I'll settle with being a *New York Times* bestselling author, thank you very much."

He laughed. "That's my Hailey. Keeping her dreams small!" He paused, then added, "So does this mean you're writing again?"

I squirmed a little at this. When I was growing up, my dad had always loved to hear my stories, which may have been partially why I loved writing so much. In fact, before I even knew how to write, I would tell him stories and he'd type them into the computer, then print them out so I could draw the pictures. Once I was older, we'd write them together, taking turns at each chapter. We once created a story that was almost a hundred pages long, about elves and princesses and fiery monsters that wanted to eat them. (The last part being Dad's contribution.)

But the last few stories I'd sent him had gone unread; he'd been too busy at work. And eventually I'd stopped sending them altogether, not wanting him to feel bad about not having the time. I guess he must have assumed I'd stopped writing entirely.

"I'm trying to enter a short-story competition," I told him. "That's one of the reasons I wanted to go to Comicpalooza in the first place." I quickly explained the contest and the writing-camp scholarship.

When I finished, I realized Dad had a worried look on his face.

"What?" I asked a little uncomfortably.

"So you've got school, homework, babysitting, and a brand-new writing project," he listed, shaking his head. "That's a lot to have on your plate, sweetheart. Are you sure you're going to have time for all of that? I don't want you to overextend yourself and fall behind. School and homework still need to take first priority, you know."

"I know," I said, my voice as indignant as I could make it, all while I forced my eyes not to drift back to the unopened history book on my desk. "Don't worry, Dad," I promised. "It's all under control; you'll see."

He nodded slowly. I could tell he really wanted to believe me. Or, perhaps more accurately, he didn't have time *not* to believe me.

A moment later he confirmed my suspicions by glancing at his watch. The time difference between China and Texas was more than twelve hours—meaning while it was nighttime here, it was tomorrow morning there.

He looked up at me. "Sorry, sweetie," he said. "I've got to get to my morning meeting. Can I call you over the weekend?"

I sighed, feeling the lump rise back to my throat again. I usually did better at controlling my emotions during these calls. But right now I just felt tired. Frustrated. Lonely. Seeing my dad looking so close, yet knowing he was so far away, just kind of got to me sometimes. Like, I could see his face, hear his voice. But that was nothing compared to having him wrap his arms around me in one of his famous bear hugs.

"When are you coming home?" I blurted out before I could stop myself. I knew he hated my asking this question. Mostly because the answer was never one I wanted to hear.

"I don't know," he said. "I'm hoping in a couple weeks—at least for a short visit."

I forced a smile at the screen, willing my eyes not to leak. A short visit. Well, that was better than nothing, right? "Sounds great," I managed to squeak out. "You'd better bring me a good present."

"Oh, I've got the best present. Just you wait and see." He smiled fondly at me. "Love you, sweetie. I'll talk to you soon."

"Love you, Dad."

And with that, the screen went blank. I stared at it for a moment, then sighed. I hopped off the bed and headed back over to my computer. I needed to start my homework before it got too late.

Instead I found myself opening up the Collin Prince story again. Starting a brand-new chapter. Where Collin has been called away on a world tour and can't be with his friends for the foreseeable future. He calls them all together one last time, to say good-bye, and they all cry and hug and promise one another they'll stay in touch—even if they're miles apart.

The words poured out of me, practically spilling onto the page, my hands barely able to keep up with the ideas in my head, washing away the writer's block in the process. I didn't stop until I'd done ten new pages—which was almost unheard of for one night. Sarah was going to be very pleased.

My teacher, on the other hand, was not.

I glanced at the clock, my mouth stretching into a

yawn. My eyes dropped down to my history book, and I wondered if I should try to stay up just a little longer. Get the assignment done. But all the energy had drained out of me at this point, and I just wanted to crawl in bed and go to sleep.

The homework would have to wait until morning.

15

"AGAIN! AGAIN! LET'S DO IT AGAIN!"

I groaned, tossing Sarah a helpless look as our two charges—four-year-old Nina and two-year-old Nora—jumped and danced around the parachute we'd been playing with. Sarah had come up with the game from her old princess babysitter—and we'd been playing "make the teddy bears fly" for the last half hour, much to their screaming and squealing delight.

"Okay, princesses," Sarah said. "But this is the *last* time." She grinned at me. She'd been saying "last time" the last five times we'd done the game. But then the kids would squeal and scream and beg, and she'd laugh and give in and start all over again. This was the first time we'd babysat for this family—and I was guessing, from the girls' reactions, it wouldn't be the last.

I had to admit, at times it was fun to be a princess. And even though most of the time we left our jobs exhausted and drained, we always looked forward to the next one. Just seeing the smiles on the kids' faces as we entered the rooms. Their wide eyes, fully buying into the magic. It made us feel magical ourselves.

Not that every job was a 100 percent win. Some kids were bratty. Some were grabby. Some would not stop asking questions all night long. Of course, all that was par for the course of any babysitting job. But as princess and pirate babysitters we had to navigate through these messy waters while staying completely in character. No matter what happened, we didn't want to destroy the magic.

Speaking of magic—we'd soon learned it was going to take some serious magic to keep our costumes from getting ripped and stained. Not to mention simply clean. When we started out, I had never considered the fact that these costumes would be dry-clean only and that they would need to be cleaned after every use, which we didn't always have time for. Since we couldn't afford the dry-cleaning bills, we would end up handwashing them and hanging them up to dry. But as the gigs started multiplying and getting closer together, sometimes we had to make a choice about whether to be a slightly damp princess—or a slightly smelly one.

Thankfully, no one had complained as of yet, and in fact our business was growing by leaps and bounds every day. At this point there was barely a day of the week where at least one of us wasn't out on a job. And while we did try to keep doubling up, there were times when we were forced to go solo, which was a lot harder and a lot less fun.

But through it all we kept our eyes on the prize. The weeks were passing quickly, and Comicpalooza was getting closer. And the way our money was rolling in, we knew we would soon have enough to start booking our tickets and hotel. When things got hard and we were tired and the last thing we wanted to do was go on another babysitting job, we'd pull up Collin Prince's photo and remind ourselves that the hard work would be worth it in the end.

"Again, again!" Nina and Nora cried. "One more time!"

This time, before Sarah could answer, we heard the

door open. I let out a breath of relief. The parents were back at last. I glanced at my phone to check the time. If I left right now, I could still get home to my room to study for an hour before dinner. Something that, between all these jobs, was getting tougher and tougher to fit into my schedule. Not to mention I still needed to work on my short story. Brody kept asking me about it, and I couldn't put him off much longer.

"So how did my little princesses do?" asked Mrs. Peterson as she walked into the room, kicking off her shoes. The little girls took one look at her and burst into tears. She raised an eyebrow. "What's wrong?" she asked.

"We don't want the princesses to leave!" cried Nina. "Please don't make them leave!"

"Hey!" I cried, dropping down to my knees. I pulled Nora to me, and Sarah followed suit with Nina. We gave them hugs and then pulled away, meeting their eyes with our own. "Don't cry," I said, tapping Nora's nose. "We can come back and play another day."

Nina sniffed, looking at Sarah suspiciously. "You promise?" she asked.

"I promise," Sarah said, leaning in to kiss her forehead. "Princess promise!" She held out her pinkie finger and showed the little girl how to lock fingers in a promise. Soon Nina was giggling.

"Princess promise!" she cried, running to her sister, trying to show her the new trick.

"Pwincess pwomise!" her sister parroted back.

Sarah and I rose to our feet and turned to Mrs. Peterson. She shook her head, looking impressed. "I have to say," she said, "usually they're begging me not to go. Now they're disappointed I'm back." She laughed. "I guess I found myself a new pair of sitters."

She reached into her pocket and pulled out a wad of cash. "Here you go," she said. "Your full fee plus a little something extra for getting them to make those giggles."

We grinned. Sarah took the money and stuffed it into her purse. "Thank you, Mrs. Peterson," she said. "And I'm pretty sure we had as much fun as they did."

We said our good-byes to the girls and headed out of the house, closing the door behind us. Sarah looked over at me, her shoulders slumping. "I just want to go sleep for a week," she confessed.

I laughed. "Me too. Who would have thought babysitting was so tiring?"

"I know, right? At least at this rate we'll have no

problems reaching our goal," Sarah said. "We just need to keep it up a little longer."

"Keep what up? Stealing other people's jobs?"

Suddenly, seemingly out of nowhere, Ginny stepped in our path. Her eyes were narrow, her brows furrowed. And her arms were crossed over her chest.

Uh-oh.

"Did you just come out of the Petersons' house?" she demanded.

I took a hesitant step backward. I'd never seen my stepsister look so furious. In fact, if looks could kill, I was pretty sure Sarah and I would have been reduced to a sloppy puddle on the sidewalk.

"What if we did?" Sarah demanded. "What business is it of yours?"

"Are you kidding me?" she cried. "I've been baby-sitting Nora and Nina since they were babies. They're my customers, not yours!"

I stared at her in shock. I'd known Ginny had done some babysitting for the family in the past, but I'd just figured she must have been busy that afternoon and had told them she couldn't make it. I had no idea they hadn't asked her in the first place.

"They *were* your customers," Sarah shot back. "Now they're ours."

"Their mother called us," I added with a shrug, trying to be diplomatic. I didn't need her to go home and tattle on me to Nancy. "Asked us if we were free. What were we supposed to say?"

"You could have said no, for a start."

"Why would we say no?"

"Geez. I don't know. Out of loyalty to your sister?"

"Oh please," Sarah interjected. "As if you wouldn't have done the exact same thing to Hailey if you had the chance. You just can't take the fact that there are newer, cooler babysitters in town now. And all the kids want us—not you."

Ginny looked as if she wanted to punch her. Instead she scowled. "Whatever," she spit out. "You're just a novelty now. Kids will be bored of your stupid costumes soon enough. Then they'll be running back to the *real* babysitters."

"If you say so," Sarah said, giving her a bright, saccharine-sweet smile. "Now if you'll excuse us, we have to go count all this *fake* babysitting money we've been earning."

And with that, she grabbed my hand and dragged me down the street. As we walked away, I stole a quick look back at Ginny, who was glaring after us with something that looked like a mixture of anger and hurt.

Sarah followed my gaze, then rolled her eyes. "It's her own fault," she declared. "If she was a good babysitter, the Petersons would never have made the switch."

I nodded slowly, though something about that didn't sit quite right. I mean, yeah, we were definitely in demand—but I wasn't sure that it was because we were actually better babysitters than the Ginnys and Jordans of the neighborhood—or that we just had cooler outfits. Did Ginny really deserve to lose out on her longtime job simply because she didn't wear a fancy dress?

"Maybe I should let her have the Peterson job back," I mused. "She *has* been doing the job for a really long time."

"Are you kidding?" Sarah cried. "Do you think she would have hesitated to steal the job from you if the situation was reversed? Besides, it's not like you stole the job from her on purpose. The mom can pick whoever she wants to babysit her kid. She's not under some kind of contract."

"I know. But . . ."

Sarah stopped in her tracks and turned to look at me. She grabbed me by the shoulders and forced me to look into her eyes. "It's called capitalism," she said. "We learned all about it in American history, remember? The fact is we're offering a superior product for a better price. And it's up to the market to decide which businesses to support. And in this case? That market is the neighborhood parents, and they have chosen us."

I nodded. I knew she was right. And feeling guilty wasn't going to help matters. And yet I still couldn't quite shake the uncomfortable feeling in the pit of my stomach. . . .

"Come on, Hailey," Sarah pleaded. "This is why you came up with this idea in the first place, right? To give us a competitive edge. Don't wimp out now that we actually have one! Now that we're so close to seeing this beautiful face in real life."

She reached into her pocket, pulled out her beloved Collin Prince cutout, unfolded it, and pushed it in my direction. I reluctantly took it, looking down at the photo. Collin seemed to smile up at me, as if to assure me everything was going to be okay.

"You're right," I said, handing back the photo. "All's

fair in love and babysitting. Now. Let's get moving. I would like to at least get in a little studying tonight."

"What? No! You promised!"

I scrunched up my face, racking my brain as to what she was talking about. *What did I promise?* "What?" I asked at last, giving up.

"To go to the library with me and work on the Collin Prince story!" she cried, looking indignant. "Do not even tell me you forgot."

I bit my lower lip. I *had* forgotten. Sarah had talked me into it a couple days ago, after I'd failed—yet again—to produce the chapter she was waiting for. From now on she wanted to work on the chapters together. Which, in my opinion, was kind of dumb. I mean, how did two people write the same story at the same time? Still, she had been so insistent, I had said yes, just to get her off my back. But now . . .

"I'm sorry," I said. "Can I get a rain check for this weekend? I've *got* to get my homework done."

"Are you serious? Hailey, do you know how hard it was to talk my mom into driving us? And now you're just going to bail on me?" She looked like she was going to cry. Or punch me. Or maybe both.

"Sarah . . ."

"Look, if you don't want to write this story with me anymore, just tell me, okay? I'll understand. But you can't keep blowing me off. It's not fair. I know it was your project to begin with, but I've put a lot of work into this story too. And it's not like I don't have homework to do as well."

"I know. I know," I assured her. "And I love writing with you, I swear. I just . . . need to get caught up first. Then I'll get back to it—I promise."

She gave me a skeptical look. I could tell she wanted desperately to believe me but wasn't so sure if she should. At last she sighed. "Okay. This weekend?" she asked. "You promise?"

"I swear on the life of Collin Prince's YouTube channel," I said, holding up my hand, as if in an oath.

She gave a small laugh at this, relieving some of the tension between us. "Okay," she said. "But you'd better show up. And you'd better have a chapter. And it better be really good. Like—Collin-pledges-his-eternal-devotion-and-offers-marriage-to-me good."

I grinned. "I think I can manage that."

16

"OH YEAH! TAKE *THAT*!"

I raised my hands in the air, one still clutching my controller. Then I scrambled to my feet and did a little victory dance around Brody, whose game character was lying on the ground, utterly annihilated, thanks to me.

He groaned, tossing his own controller on the table. "I have to admit," he said, "you are quite the gamer girl."

"I am quite the *gamer*," I corrected. "The girl part is irrelevant, seeing how I just kicked your boy butt."

He grinned. "Good point." He grabbed his controller again. "Of course that's not going to happen a second time."

"Oh, you think so? Well, bring it, Gamer Guy. Just

bring it." I dropped back down to a sitting position as he loaded up the first-person shooter we'd been playing for another go. It was Sunday afternoon, and Brody had come over this morning after I'd finished writing the Collin Prince chapter for Sarah, and we'd been playing games in the living room for the last two hours. It felt good, after all the recent stress, to just relax and have fun. Even if it was only temporary.

"This is the last time, though," I added. "After this round, I gotta get ready for my babysitting gig."

He groaned, leaning against the couch and staring up at the ceiling. "Seriously?" he said. "Another one?"

"I can't help it if we're that popular."

He shook his head, turning back to the TV, where the game was starting again. "If this business keeps growing, we're going to run out of time to play video games."

I snorted, maneuvering my character up onto a bridge, where I could hopefully catch him coming through the canyon. He wasn't wrong; I barely had time for anything anymore. It seemed like every time I had a free afternoon, someone would call or text, asking us to come over and watch their kids. And while the money was great, the lack of free time was starting to really stink.

Like now, for example, when I wanted nothing more than to hang out with Brody and play video games and eat snacks all afternoon. Instead I'd have to head upstairs, put on a fancy dress, and do my hair. Spend an hour getting ready before heading over to actually do the job. Basically ruining the rest of the afternoon.

"It's just temporary," I reminded him (as well as myself). "Just until we have enough money saved for the convention. Then we can quit for good."

"I suppose it *is* for a good cause," Brody agreed, his eyes glued to the screen as he attempted to track my character down. "You can talk all about it someday when you win your first Pulitzer Prize. Hailey Smith—*New York Times* bestselling author—started out from humble roots of princess babysitting."

I laughed, and it turned into a yawn. I hadn't gotten very good sleep last night. Or for the past few nights, actually. I had set my alarm early this morning to make sure I got that chapter done for Sarah—before she decided to hunt me down in real life. And I planned to spend tonight—after the kids went to bed—studying for tomorrow's big test. What was it they said? No rest for the wicked?

Or the wicked awesome, as the case might be.

"Are you going to take a pen name when you're rich and famous?" Brody added, glancing over at me for a moment before his eyes returned to the screen.

"Sure. I'll call myself H. K. Rowling. Then, if I'm lucky, someone will get confused and buy my books instead of Harry Potter. I'll make millions of dollars from their mistake."

"Yeah, but what if someone buys Harry Potter instead of your book by mistake?" Brody asked. "After all, you have no idea how popular you're going to be. J. K. could be trying to steal sales from *you*."

"Oh yeah. I'm sure she's shaking in her boots at the possibility." I snorted, steering my character off the bridge, bored of waiting for him to find me. Time to go track him down.

"Speaking of, how's the story going?" he asked. "You haven't been too busy to work on it, have you?"

About that. I swallowed hard.

"Oh no. Of course not. The story takes first priority," I tried to say brightly. "And it's coming out great. Really . . . great."

I wondered if I sounded at all believable. Or just tired. Or maybe like I was lying through my teeth?

In truth, I hadn't worked on the story in almost a week. I'd been too busy, too exhausted, and, lately, altogether too frustrated.

Not that Brody needed to know that.

I glanced over at him. His lips had curled into a smile. "Glad to hear it," he said. "Because I've got great news."

"Oh?"

"I asked my dad, and he's agreed to look at it before you send it in to the contest."

Wait, what?

I hit the controller with my thumb and the screen spun. Brody's character jumped out of nowhere, taking me down. I stared at my character's corpse on the screen and groaned as the real-life Brody jumped up to do a victory lap around my living room.

"Who's the gamer *now*?" he cheered.

I collapsed onto the floor. "You're such a cheater!" I cried. "You can't just say something like that and then jump out at me!"

He grinned impishly. "Sorry," he said, looking anything but. Then he winked. "Best two out of three?"

I glanced at the clock on the wall. I was running out of time. But still . . .

"Duh," I said. "Prepare to get royally stomped."

He dropped down to the floor again and grabbed his controller. I pressed the buttons to reset the match. "So go back," I said, as the game loaded. "Your dad wants to read *my* story?"

Brody grinned widely, obviously pleased with himself. "Sorry," he said. "Maybe I should have asked you first. But I told him about how you wanted to enter it in the Comicpalooza contest and how it was really important that you win. He said if you wanted, you could send it to him and he could give you a few pointers." He shrugged. "Not that I'm sure it isn't already awesome . . ."

I bit my lower lip. It wasn't already awesome. In fact, it barely even existed. Just a few paragraphs I'd jotted down weeks ago and hadn't been able to continue with since. Every day I would sit down at my computer to try to work on it. Opening up the Word document and reading over what I had already written. Then I'd usually end up deleting half of it—realizing that what I'd thought was pretty good the day before was actually garbage. Which made for very little progress and a lot of frustration.

I realized Brody was still waiting for an answer. "What do I think?" I stammered. "I think that's amazing. I don't know what to say. Um, thank you! Thank you so much. You really didn't have to do that."

"I wanted to," Brody assured me. "After all, I know how important this all is to you. You've been working so hard, doing all these babysitting jobs just to get to the convention so you can enter the contest. You deserve to have every chance to win."

"Thank you," I said at last. "I really appreciate it. And I will get the story to you as soon as it's ready. I just need a few more days to polish it up. Then I'll send it over to you so you can forward it to your dad." I paused, then added, "Also, you're dead again."

"What? NO!" he cried in dismay as I unleashed my full force on him. He dropped the controller in his lap, sighing loudly. "Completely unfair."

"Completely, absolutely fair," I corrected. "Now, sorry, but I really must get ready."

"Get ready for what?"

I looked up to realize my stepmother had poked her head into the living room. I scrambled to my feet. "Oh. I have a babysitting job in an hour," I told her.

To my surprise, her face creased into a scowl. "Since when?"

"Um, since last night? Don't worry—it's just for the Jacksons down the street. So I don't need a ride." My stepmother had been complaining lately that I was using her as a taxi service for all my various jobs. Thankfully, this one wouldn't be an issue.

But, to my dismay, her frown didn't lift. "Hailey, you were supposed to stay home this afternoon to let the plumber in, remember?"

"Oh." I squinted at her. "I was?"

"Yes. You were. We talked about it at length on Wednesday. I have my board meeting for the Saint Francis group. It's very important that I be there this afternoon. I told you this, remember? You said it wouldn't be a problem."

I winced, starting to remember. "Can't the plumber come later?" I asked. "I really can't just bail on Mrs. Jackson last minute."

"You shouldn't have told her you could babysit in the first place," my stepmother shot back, her voice now raised in anger. "You had a commitment here at home."

"I know. But I forgot. Can't Ginny stay home?"

"No. She can't. Ginny has her study group. And anyway, she shouldn't have to ruin her afternoon because you double-booked yourself."

She looked really angry now. I bit my lower lip. *Stupid, Hailey. How could you forget something like that?*

"You know, this babysitting thing is getting to be too much," my stepmother added, evidently now on a rampage. "I didn't say anything when it was just a couple hours a week. But now it's like you're busy every day. You have some responsibilities to this family, young lady, not to mention your schoolwork. And if you can't live up to those, then you're going to have to stop babysitting altogether."

Panic seized me. "No!" I cried. "Look. I'm sorry. I just forgot. That's all. It won't happen again."

I realized Brody had come up behind me. "I can wait for the plumber," he told my stepmother.

She looked at him. "Sweetie, that's nice of you. But you don't have to do that."

"I don't mind," he said. "It'll give me an excuse to get some more PlayStation time in. Just let me know what I need to tell him when he gets here and I'll take care of it."

My stepmother pursed her lips. I could tell she

wanted to argue—to say it was my mistake and I should take responsibility. But at the same time, she needed someone to meet the plumber, and Brody was the only one who could do it.

Finally she sighed. "Fine," she said. "Thank you, Brody. I'll show you the toilet that's been giving us problems."

As she led him away, she stopped at the door, turning around to give me a look. A look that told me exactly how much I had disappointed her.

A look that I was starting to know all too well.

17

"AHOY, YE LOUSY LANDLUBBERS, IT'S TIME FOR ALL HANDS ON deck!" Madison cried, dancing around the living room, waving her plastic sword in the air. She was a little out of breath from doing her show, but she hid it nicely.

"The deck, in this case, being your beds," I clarified from my position on the couch, in case either of the boys wasn't fluent in piratespeak. As backup pirate princess tonight I had put on one of the less . . . *large* princess dresses we'd picked up at the thrift store. It wasn't as impressive as my ball gown, but I had to admit, it was nice to sometimes babysit with full lung capacity.

Madison lunged at the boys. They shrieked and

ducked out of her grasp, running for the other side of the room and hiding behind the kitchen table.

"Aw," cried the older one. "But we want to find more treasure first!"

"Yeah!" cried his little brother. "More tweh-shore!"

Madison shook her head sternly. "There will be time for treasure another day. A good pirate knows when to batten down the hatches and get a good night's sleep. To live to fight another day." She gave them a knowing wink. "But if you're good, you may find a little something special under your pillows—to light the treasure map of your dreams."

The boys exchanged curious looks, then raced upstairs, practically tripping over each other to get there first. I glanced over at Madison questioningly. She grinned. "Glow sticks," she said. "Their parents left them for us in case we needed to resort to bribery. Which, clearly, we do."

The cries of excitement coming from upstairs soon confirmed her words. "You make a good pirate," I told her.

"You make a pretty decent princess yourself," she shot back with a smile. "Now let's get these scallywags to bed so we can pop the popcorn their parents left us and watch movies. All this adventure has left me starving."

"I'll eat the popcorn," I said with a sigh. "But no movie for me. I am dreadfully behind in my homework."

I rose from the couch, and together we headed upstairs, where the boys were brushing their teeth, now eager to get under the covers to play with their new glow toys. I just hoped the excitement of the "treasure" wouldn't keep them awake until their parents got home.

Once we had tucked them in and said good night—with a stern warning from Dread Pirate Madison not to get out of bed except for an emergency—we headed downstairs to start the popcorn. The boys' parents had promised to be home by nine, meaning we had about an hour to kill.

Or, you know, prevent me from flunking out of school.

Large bag of popcorn in hand, Madison settled down in front of the TV, flicking through the Netflix options. She finally settled on *Pirates of the Caribbean*. (To get some inspiration, she said, though she already had her pirate act down to a science. I think she just wanted to stare at Orlando Bloom.)

She set down the remote and stretched her hands above her head. "This is the life," she said. "Getting paid to eat and watch movies." Then she turned to me. "This isn't going to distract you from your homework, is it? 'Cause I can go into another room. I think there was a TV in the den."

I waved her off. "I'm fine," I assured her. "I can watch and study."

"And finish the next chapter of the Collin Prince adventure?" she teased, her eyes sparkling. 'Cause I'm pretty sure Sarah said something about resorting to decapitation if you didn't produce something new this weekend."

"I happen to have sent her a chapter this morning, thank you very much. And if she decapitates me? That'll be the very last one."

"Good point. Not sure she's seeing things that clearly, though."

I groaned. "Sometimes I wish I'd never started that story," I said.

"What?" Madison frowned, turning to me. "But it's so good. Sure, I don't get as into it as much as Sarah. But I love reading it. You're really talented, Hailey. I bet you could even write a real book someday—if you wanted to. And get it published."

I forced myself to nod, but I couldn't prevent the sinking feeling that dropped in my stomach at her words. I knew that she was trying to be encouraging. That she had no idea how much I had been struggling. But still—her blind confidence stung.

I sighed. "Look. I love that everyone loves the Collin Prince story. But I have to take a break. With all the babysitting . . . and . . . stuff, I've gotten crazy behind. And if my grades drop? My dad's going to long-distance decapitate me himself."

Madison gave me a sympathetic look. "Oh, I hear you," she said. "I mean, this babysitting stuff is awesome for making money. But I've had to miss a couple practices, and Coach is threatening to bench me if I miss any more." She sighed. "In fact, you know that job you have me set up for on Thursday? Can you possibly get Sarah or Kalani to do it? I just realized I have an away game."

I pulled up the calendar on my phone. "Looks like Sarah has dance that night," I said. "And Kalani has some kind of family thing going on." I shrugged. "I guess I could do it myself."

"Thanks." Madison looked relieved. "I'd really appreciate that."

I made the adjustment in the calendar, my stomach twisting a little as I did. I had a big project due for my English class on that Friday after. But I could probably knock it out on Tuesday or Wednesday. . . . It wasn't ideal, but it would be worse to cancel on the parents altogether. We'd end up losing them as customers, and they might tell other parents as well.

I closed the calendar and looked up. "Okay," I said. "We're all set. Now I really need to start looking at this—"

A loud bang interrupted my words, followed by a long wail—coming from upstairs. Madison and I leaped out of our seats, just in time to see Noah run to the landing.

"What's wrong?" Madison demanded.

"It's Liam," he said. "He's stuck in the toilet."

Madison shot me a look. "What do you mean . . . stuck in the toilet?" she asked. I could tell she was wondering if this was just another excuse to get out of bed or if she should take it seriously. One thing we'd learned from these babysitting jobs was how creative kids could be when coming up with reasons they shouldn't be in bed. From drinks and snacks to going to the potty to needing a back rub or a night-light . . .

They'd all make great lawyers someday.

"Uh, well . . ." Noah looked sheepish. "We were just playing and I threw his glow stick and it landed in the toilet just as he was trying to flush. So he reached in the toilet and tried to grab it and his arm got stuck."

I sighed, setting my homework on the couch. "I'll go check on them," I told Madison. "You deal with the popcorn." She nodded and I trudged upstairs, thankful once again I'd worn the shorter, easier-to-manage princess dress.

"Where is he?" I asked Noah when I reached the top of the stairs. He grabbed my hand and dragged me to the bathroom, where, sure enough, his brother was leaning over the toilet, one arm stuck down inside.

I rolled my eyes. "You guys will do anything not to go to sleep, won't you?" I dropped down to my knees and grabbed Liam's arm, tugging on it to free it from the toilet.

But it didn't budge.

I bit my lower lip. Tried again, tugging harder this time. I didn't want to hurt him, but I couldn't just leave him like this either. "Can you just wiggle your hand a little?" I asked Liam. But he just shook his head, looking scared.

"What if I have to pee?" Noah demanded. "Do I pee on his arm?" He paused, then added, with a wicked grin, "What if I have to poop?"

Liam burst into tears. "Don't poop on me!" he begged his brother.

I groaned. "No one's peeing or pooping on anyone," I assured them. "You have a second bathroom downstairs, you know."

"Yeah, but what if I can't hold it?" Noah asked, looking far too delighted for his own good. I gave him a scolding look.

"Stop teasing your brother. And go tell Madison to come up here. I need her."

To his credit, Noah did as he was told, and a moment later I could hear Madison's footsteps on the stairs. She popped her head into the bathroom, her eyes widening when she saw Liam.

"Is he really stuck?" she asked.

I rose to my feet, grabbed her, and pulled her out of the room. No need to scare Liam more than he already was. "He's really stuck," I said, my heart pounding nervously now. "What should we do?"

"Let's try together," Madison suggested.

The two of us returned to the bathroom, bright, fake smiles pasted on our faces. "So, Liam, we're going to just try again, okay?" I asked.

He whimpered and nodded. I grabbed his upper arm. Madison grabbed the lower. Together on the count of three we pulled.

But he was stuck fast.

18

i STARED AT THE TOILET, THEN UP AT MADISON. SHE STARED
back at me with a look of horror that I was pretty sure
matched my own look.

"What are we going to do?" she asked.

"I don't know. We can't just leave him there." I swallowed hard. "I think we need to call his parents."

"No!" Madison's eyes widened in horror. "They'll
think we're the worst babysitters ever!"

I glanced over at Liam. "They might not be wrong."

"No." Madison shook her head. "There has to be
another way." She was quiet for a moment, thinking.
Then: "I know! My uncle Mike is a fireman!"

"So? He's stuck in a toilet. Not on fire."

"I know. But firemen help people who are stuck. Like cats in a tree."

I gave her a skeptical look. She waved me off. "Seriously, Hailey. He will totally be able to help us." She reached into her pocket, pulled out her phone, and dialed a number.

I turned to Liam. "Help is on the way," I assured him. "Do you want a cookie while you're waiting?"

Liam indeed wanted a cookie. As Madison explained the situation to her uncle on the phone, I walked downstairs to get him one. My heart was still beating nervously in my chest. Could a fireman really get him free? What if they had to break the toilet to do it? His parents were so not going to be happy if they came home to a broken toilet. How much did a new toilet cost, anyway? What if they made us pay for it—using our savings for Comicpalooza?

Five minutes later we heard a siren outside. Noah ran to the window, flush with excitement. "This is so cool!" he cried. "A real-life fire truck!" He pressed his face against the glass. "Ooh! Make that *three* fire trucks!"

Three fire trucks? I bit my lower lip. Were *three* fire trucks really necessary? Three fire trucks making siren noises, for that matter? I mean, I thought we were trying to keep a low profile here, not put the whole neighborhood on alert!

The doorbell rang and Madison ran to answer it. She swung it open and let her uncle—and his three fireman friends—through the door. They were dressed in full-on fire gear, including hats. One of them had an actual ax. Noah looked as if he was going to pass out from excitement. I wanted to pass out too. But for a much different reason.

The firemen looked us up and down, confused looks on their faces. "Costume party?" one of them asked.

"Something like that," Madison replied. "Now come on. He's in the upstairs bathroom! Hurry!"

They all four ran upstairs, leaving the front door open, the lights still flashing on the three trucks outside. I wondered if it would be rude to ask them to turn them off before the rescue—you know, so as not to cause more of a scene than we already had. Hopefully they'd be quick.

I followed them upstairs, trying to keep Noah at a safe distance, which wasn't easy. As the firemen crowded around the bathroom door, I could hear them talking to

Liam. But I couldn't see what they were doing. I paced the hall, waiting, hoping. Feeling pretty helpless, too. What were we going to do if they couldn't get him free?

"What's going on? Why are the firemen here? Is there a fire? Where's the fire?"

I whirled around, my eyes bulging as I caught Mr. and Mrs. Jackson running up the stairs, their faces white and horrified. Oh no! Worst timing ever!

"It's fine," I tried to tell them, but my shaky voice was probably not all that convincing. "It's not a fire. It's—"

"Liam's stuck in the toilet!" Noah interrupted proudly. "The firemen are here to get him out!"

"What?" Both parents turned to stare at me. I felt my face go bright red. "Um, yeah," I said. At this point there was no sense in denying it. "I was, uh, about to call you?"

Mrs. Jackson didn't reply, just pushed past me, making her way toward the bathroom. Before she could squeeze her way through, Liam stepped out, smiling widely. His arm was red but intact.

"Here he is!" Uncle Mike proclaimed, ruffling the kid's hair. "All free. Didn't even have to cut off any fingers to do it!" he teased. Which, in my opinion, was so not funny.

"Liam!" his mother scolded. "What did I tell you about sticking your hand in the toilet?"

Liam scowled. "It was Noah's fault. He threw my glow stick in there!"

His mother sighed, straightening back to her feet. She turned to the firemen. "Thank you for getting him out," she said.

They tipped their hats. "All in a day's work, ma'am," said Uncle Mike. "You're just lucky you had such resourceful babysitters. Most kids would have panicked and pulled him too hard—which could have hurt his arm. They were smart to call professionals."

Mrs. Jackson turned to us, nodding slowly. "I guess you're right. Thank you, girls," she said. "It's good to know the boys were in good hands."

"Oh, it was nothing," Madison said, waving her off. "All in a day's work for Princesses and Pirates, Incorporated."

I nodded meekly, my heart still thudding hard in my chest.

All in a day's work . . . but hopefully never again.

19

WHILE IT WAS SAFE TO SAY THE JACKSONS WERE NOT SUPER thrilled that their four-year-old son had spent a portion of his evening with his hand stuck in a toilet, they thankfully didn't blame us for allowing it to happen. In fact, they actually apologized for Liam's behavior. (Evidently the kid had a bit of a history of sticking his arm into places it didn't belong and getting stuck because of it.) Apologized *and* gave us a fifty-dollar tip for "doing the right thing." *That* made Madison feel a whole lot better.

I would have felt better too, had the incident not completely destroyed my chance to study for tomorrow's test. Now it was after nine. My stepmother would freak out about my getting home this late on a school night—no way was she going to allow me to stay up even later, especially since she was already mad at me about the plumber thing. I could tell she was *this close* to cracking down on my babysitting altogether, and I couldn't let that happen. Not when we were so close to earning enough money for our trip.

And so I went to sleep without studying, setting my alarm for super early the next day. I figured I could at least read over my notes then and maybe have a chance to score a B or something. No big deal.

Instead I tossed and turned most of the night, and when I did sleep, I was treated to nightmarish visions of toilets with big teeth chasing me through the house. It wasn't until nearly dawn that I finally passed out cold—and then I ended up sleeping through my alarm. My stepmother had to wake me up and harass me into getting dressed. In the end I barely made the bus and missed breakfast altogether. By the time I got to my history class, I was tired, hungry, and completely unprepared. And as the questions seemed to swim across the page to my bleary eyes, I realized there was no way I'd be getting a B today. In fact, I'd be lucky if I passed at all.

Madison looked just as exhausted as I was when I

found her at lunch. Evidently, she hadn't gotten much sleep either. As I sat down at the table, I watched as she picked listlessly at her food, for once in her life seemingly not hungry.

"Where's Sarah?" I asked, looking around.

"Called in sick," she replied, not looking up. "Which is what I should have done," she added. "Seeing that I was up all night." She groaned loudly, rubbing her eyes with her fists. "I am going to be a total wreck at my game tonight."

I stifled a grimace. Madison was the star pitcher on her softball team. If she was off her game (no pun intended), it could cost the team their coveted first-place ranking and eventual spot in the playoffs.

"Just eat a lot of chocolate before the game," I advised her. "I hear it has caffeine." I pushed my brownie at her. "Here. You can start now."

I hated giving up a brownie. But it would be even worse to be indirectly responsible for Chase Junior High losing out on making the playoffs. At least I deserved to get a bad grade on my test. Madison's teammates, on the other hand, were innocent parties to all this.

"Do you think maybe we're doing too much?"

Madison asked, picking out the chocolate chips from the brownie. She chewed them for a moment, then yawned loudly. "Babysitting, school, sports. I feel like I barely have enough time to comb my hair anymore."

I frowned. "It's just temporary," I reminded her. "Until we get enough money for Comicpalooza. Then we can cut back. Maybe even stop altogether if we want to."

"Stop what altogether?" Kalani asked, sitting down at the table, lunch tray in hand.

"Babysitting," Madison and I answered in unison.

"What? We can't stop now!" Kalani protested. "Not when we're so close to our goal!"

"Actually, we're only about halfway there," Madison corrected.

"Exactly! Halfway! Which means we only have halfway to go," Kalani cried. "Glass half full, people. Glass half full!"

"Do you how many babysitting jobs that is?" Madison shook her head. "I'm sorry. I just don't think I can keep this up. If I get kicked off the team, then I won't be able to try out for the varsity team next year in high school. Even the chance to see Collin Prince isn't worth that."

Kalani looked horrified. "How can you say that?" she demanded. "This is Collin Prince we're talking about here! He is worth *every* sacrifice."

Madison's face twisted. She'd looked tired before. Now she just looked angry. "That's just stupid and you know it," she snapped.

"Well, maybe I think *you're* the—"

"Guys! Please!" I interrupted, jumping between them. "Let's not fight, okay? We're all on the same side, after all. I know you're exhausted, Madison. I am too. And Kalani, no one's giving up. I promise. We just need to . . . slow down a little. Madison, you can take the week off. Get some sleep. Get caught up. I'll take your jobs."

Even as I said the words, I mentally tried to add up in my head how much extra babysitting that would be. But I forced myself to push the thought aside. I'd make it work . . . somehow. Otherwise Madison would mutiny and the entire dream would be over forever. All the work we'd put in so far—for nothing.

Madison stared down at her plate, at first not responding. Then she nodded slowly. "I guess that'd be okay," she said. Then she looked up at me. "But are you sure you want to do that, Hail? No offense, but you kind of look like death warmed over yourself."

"I'm fine," I assured her, trying to give her my best *not dead yet* look. "You worry about softball, and when you feel ready, you can come back. Even if it's just on weekends. We started this whole thing together, and we're going to end it together. And seriously, it won't be for much longer, I promise."

"Okay," Madison said. "We'll try it this way. But if anything else happens? I'm sorry, but I'm going to have to bail for good." She gave me a rueful look. "I love Collin Prince. And I love you guys even more. But I can't bet my entire future on some celebrity sighting."

I could hear Kalani grunt next to me, but I refused to look at her. "You won't have to," I promised Madison. "It's all going to work out. You'll see."

"Okay." Madison rose to her feet and grabbed her tray. "I'm going to go find a corner in the library to steal a nap before lunch is over," she said. "I'll catch you guys later."

She gave us a salute, then walked out of the cafeteria. Finally I allowed myself to turn to Kalani.

"She won't quit," I assured her. "It'll be fine. You'll see."

Kalani sighed. I held up my hand to give her a high

five. She returned it with something less than her usual enthusiasm. Giving her what I hoped was a reassuring smile, I rose to my feet and headed to the trash to dump my own mostly uneaten lunch. Even though I'd skipped breakfast, I just didn't feel hungry anymore.

In truth, I was too worried.

20

THAT NIGHT, I STARED AT THE COMPUTER SCREEN. THE BLANK page stared back at me, as if mocking me with its emptiness. I groaned, scrubbing my face with my hands. Why, oh why had I told Brody I was almost done with this story? When in reality I'd barely even started it? Now he was expecting me to send him something this week to give to his father to read. Which was such a huge opportunity—I didn't want to miss out. But try as I might, I couldn't come up with anything I wanted to say.

Sighing, I flipped documents. Maybe I could just work a tiny bit on the new Collin Prince chapter—just to get my creative juices flowing. Sarah had emailed me two more chapters that afternoon—she must not have been *that* sick after all—and was now impatiently waiting for me to write my next part. Maybe once I did that I'd be all warmed up—and could switch back to the contest story or something.

Sarah let out a gasp as Collin Prince collapsed in front of her. He looked up at her with his wide brown eyes. "I need your help," he whispered in a hoarse voice.

Her heart melted. She took him into her arms. "Of course," she whispered. "Just tell me wwwwwwwwwwhkghkwhd'ojwj;ljlkjfop'aej aejfegjaeffafeavfdvsdggfsdfsgfdgfS

"Hailey? Hailey! Wake up!"

"Five more minutes," I begged, trying to pull the covers back over my head to drown out my stepmother's nagging voice. It took me a moment to realize there were no covers. Because I wasn't in bed.

"Not five more *seconds*," my stepmother scolded, barging into my bedroom. She raised an eyebrow as she looked at me at my desk. "The bus will be here in ten minutes, and I'm subbing at the high school today, so I can't drive you if you miss it. I need you to get up, *now*."

I blinked my eyes. The inside of my mouth tasted fuzzy—like it was stuffed with cotton. My head was spinning and my stomach was churning. I looked up and realized I must have fallen asleep at my desk. With my head on the keyboard, judging from the long string of garbage typing that filled the screen.

Oh no.

Suddenly I was wide awake. I tried to remember the night before, but the memories were all cloudy. How could I have fallen asleep? I never fell asleep at my desk.

But I had. And I'd lost an entire night. The one night this week I didn't have a babysitting job. The night I was supposed to get caught up on my homework. Write my short story. Continue the Collin Prince saga. Sarah was going to kill me. My teachers were going to flip out. Brody—Brody was going to know I lied to him.

I forced myself to suck in a shaky breath. *Focus, Hailey.* After all, panicking wasn't going to help matters. I rose from my seat and stumbled around the room, searching for something suitable to wear to school. *Priority number one: Don't miss the bus.*

But just as I slipped a T-shirt over my head, I heard

a squealing noise outside my window. I ran and pushed aside the curtains, just in time to see my bus pull away from the curb.

Of course. The one morning the driver was actually on time.

A moment later my stepmother marched into my room again. Now she looked really angry. "I don't have time for this," she growled. "I don't know what's going on with you, but you need to get your act together, young lady." She huffed. "We'll talk later. For now I'll have Ginny drive you so you won't be late."

"No!" I protested. No way was I going to sit in the car with Ginny. She'd probably drive me over a cliff at this point, she was so mad at me about the babysitting thing. "I mean, that's okay. I'll walk or something."

"It's five miles, Hailey. You'd never make it in time."

"Then I'll take an Uber."

"An Uber we will have to pay for? That's ridiculous, Hailey...."

Argh. Couldn't she just leave me alone? "Okay, okay! Fine. I'll let Ginny drive me. Whatever."

"Oh. You'll *let* her drive you, will you?" my stepmother repeated. Her face twisted. "Why how *generous* of Your Majesty to *let* your sister go out of her way to do a favor." Her eyes narrowed in on me. "You know what, Hailey? You need to start acting a little more grateful for what this family does for you. And start treating your sister with some respect."

I glowered at her, anger burning through me like a fire. Respect? Like Ginny treated *me* with respect? Like *anyone* treated me with respect in this house?

"She's not my sister," I snapped back. "And I never asked to be part of this family. Go yell at my dad if you're unhappy with me being here—after all, he's the one who dumped me on you in the first place."

I felt tears swim to my eyes and angrily tried to brush them away. It was so unfair. If only Dad were here. He could drive me to school like he used to when I was little. I remembered how we used to swing by the coffee shop on the way there and buy a chocolate coconut donut to split between us. We'd laugh as the crumbs got all over the car—no matter how careful we tried to be. And then my dad would declare loudly, "No more coconut donuts ever!" But by the next week he'd forget and order another—just as crumbly.

I looked up, realizing my stepmother was still

standing there, the strangest expression on her face. Suddenly I felt bad about my outburst. After all, it wasn't her fault that she was stuck with me. She probably thought she'd been escaping single-parent duties when she married my dad—only to end up having her work doubled.

I sighed. "Look, I'm sorry. I didn't mean—"

But she just shook her head and walked out of the room, slamming the door a little too hard behind her. For a moment I just stared at the door, my chest tight. Then I slumped my shoulders and finished getting dressed. I'd have to apologize to her tonight. Tell her I didn't mean it. That I was just tired. And grumpy. And stressed.

I had barely finished getting my socks and shoes on when Ginny showed up. She entered my room without knocking (of course) and looked down at me, as if I were something she'd just scraped off the bottom of her shoe.

"I hear you need a ride to school," she said.

"Yeah. Thanks," I muttered.

She cocked her head, giving me a suspiciously innocent look. "For what?"

Argh. She was going to milk this for all it was worth, wasn't she? "For the ride," I said, straightening up. "Thank you for the ride."

"Oh. But I'm not giving you a ride."

"What? But Nancy said . . ."

"Mom's already gone to work. Sorry."

"Come on, Ginny," I begged, now feeling a little scared. What was I going to do if she really wouldn't take me? "You know I don't have any other way to get there."

"Well, maybe you can you use all that money you have from stealing my babysitting jobs and call yourself a cab."

I drew in a breath, trying to keep my voice steady. "I didn't steal your babysitting jobs," I replied. "It's not my fault the kids' mother called me instead of you."

"Which you didn't even bother to tell me about. I had to catch you leaving their house."

I squirmed a little. "Look, I'm sorry. It was nothing personal, I swear. We just needed the money."

"Of course. While the rest of us babysit out of the goodness of our hearts."

"What's that supposed to mean?"

"It means, my little self-absorbed sister, you're not the only one in this family who needs money." Her voice cracked a little at the last part. I stared at her, puzzled.

"What do you need money for?" I asked in a quiet voice.

She opened her mouth, then shut it again. Giving me a look that felt like daggers straight to my heart. Then, at last, she shook her head, dropping her gaze.

"You know, I can't believe I once thought it'd be cool to have a sister," she muttered. Then she looked up at me. "Have fun finding a way to school," she spit out before turning on her heel and stomping out the door. I watched her go, my tongue tied, not knowing what to say. For a moment she'd looked so upset. Like she was going to cry. But why? What did she have to be upset about?

What did she need money for?

I shook my head. It was probably nothing. She probably just wanted a new pair of leggings or something dumb like that and wanted to make me feel guilty.

I sighed. Well, mission accomplished.

I looked around the room, suddenly feeling really weary. I reached for my phone and scrolled through my contacts list, trying to decide who to call for a ride. I tried Sarah first, then Madison, but neither answered their phones. They must have already been at school. Kalani might have hers on, but she always took the bus 'cause her parents left early for work. I could try Brody, but then he'd ask me about the story and I'd have to go and lie again. And even if he was able to get me to school, then I would have to deal with my teachers and my unfinished homework.

I dropped down onto my bed. Okay, then. Sick day it was. I was actually feeling pretty sick to my stomach at this point anyway, so it technically wasn't a lie.

Yes, I decided, feeling a little better. I would stay home. I would use the day to catch up. Finish my homework. Write the short story. Maybe even do a little chapter for Sarah with Collin Prince. And then—

I let out a big yawn. But first I could catch up on some sleep.

I kicked off my shoes, put my pj pants back on, and slid back into bed. I'd just sleep a little. Then I'd start working. I'd work all day. Until it was time for the babysitting gig at the Valdezes' tonight. Which I needed to fix my dress for—it had gotten kind of torn up two babysitting jobs ago during an intense princess-pirate battle we'd staged. But I would have plenty of time for that. . . .

21

i WAS AWOKEN SOMETiME LATER BY AN iNCESSANT BANGiNG
at my door. I groaned, rolling over, blearily looking over
at my bedside alarm clock, wondering who would be
trying to interrupt my sleep at this hour.

Until I realized exactly what hour it was.

Five p.m.

I had slept all day.

The knock came again.

"I'm up!" I cried, trying to dash out of bed, as if to
look like I hadn't been sound asleep only seconds before.
But I only managed to get my foot tangled in one of my
blankets, which sent me crashing to the floor.

My stepmother burst into the room. "What are you

doing?" she demanded, looking down at me, sprawled out crookedly on the floor.

I winced, rubbing my knee. "Would you believe me if I said yoga?"

She didn't reply. Just handed me the house phone. The one we barely ever used, seeing as we all had our own cells. "Hailey, your friend Kalani is on the phone. She says you never showed up to the babysitting job you were supposed to do with her today."

My eyes widened. Oh no! I'd slept through the job at the Valdez house? I grabbed the phone. "Kalani?" I asked.

"Where are you?" she demanded. "I am literally being killed by children. Like, their parents are going to come home to find a dead babysitter in their master bathroom. You need to get here now! You're two hours late!"

I bit my lower lip, glancing up at my stepmother, who was glaring at me suspiciously. "Um, sure," I said, turning back to the phone. "I'm sorry; I'm on my way. I'll be right there. I just have to put my dress on and—"

"Forget the dress! The dress will take too long. I need you now!"

"But that's sort of our—"

"*Now, Hailey.* Or I will seriously never talk to you

again!" I could hear a crashing sound in the background and cringed.

I hung up the phone and handed it back to my stepmother. "Um. Can I get a ride to the Valdezes'?" I asked. "I don't really have time to walk since—"

"Did you even go to school today?" she demanded, looking around the room.

"Of course I did!" I cried, grabbing a pair of jeans off the floor. "What would make you think that I didn't go to school today?"

Nancy's eyes narrowed. "For one thing you're still wearing the pajama pants you wore to bed last night."

I cringed. *Busted.* For a split second I entertained the idea of telling her it was pajama day at school today, but then decided it would be too easy for her to check to see if I was lying.

"Look. Can we talk about my bad choices in fashion later?" I begged. "I need to go rescue Kalani."

She opened her mouth, looking like she wanted to object, but finally gave in. "Okay," she snapped. "But we are talking about this the second you get home."

"Sure. No problem. Whatever. Now can you give me that ride?"

* * *

I arrived at the Valdez house twenty minutes later and helped Kalani wrestle the kids into submission. It wasn't easy. And they were especially disappointed that I wasn't in costume.

"Mommy said we were getting *two* princesses to play with!" objected four-year-old Addison, who was dressed in a wicked witch costume.

"Yeah!" added her five-year-old sister, Ava, who was dressed as Snow White. "*You're* not a princess. You didn't even brush your hair."

My hands went to my hair. Man—I knew I had forgotten something.

"Or her teeth," Kalani muttered.

O-kay. Make that two somethings.

"Um, actually," I said, trying to think quickly, "I *am* a princess. It's just sometimes we princesses like to wear jeans—like everyone else. You know, like casual Friday."

"It's Tuesday," Ava pointed out.

"Right. Casual Tuesday. Totally a thing in princess land," I agreed with a nervous laugh. "In fact, it's my clever disguise. You see, I'm the lost princess and . . ."

I trailed off, realizing I had started telling two

different stories at once from the scripts we'd made up: the princess in disguise (who knew of her royal birth but was hiding out from bad guys) and the lost princess (who didn't know she was a princess until she discovered her prince). (The casual Tuesday thing wasn't part of either—just desperate me making stuff up on the fly.) To be fair, my brain was all mushy from sleeping all day, and I was lucky I remembered any of our scripts at this point.

I could feel Kalani giving me the evil eye. "Don't listen to her. She's *not* a princess at all," she told Addison and Ava in a confidential tone. "She's actually just a poor little maid. *Our* poor maid. And she's going to do *whatever* we tell her to do." She gave me a look that told me I'd better not even think about arguing. "Now," she pronounced with a smug smile, "let's talk dishes."

Oh dear.

The dishes, it turned out, were only the beginning of my punishment. I was also made to clean up the mess the kids had created earlier in their playroom, dust the entire house, and finally sweep the floor. Kalani, still in character, even managed to turn it into a game, having the kids yell at me if I missed a spot. Fun times. But I kept my mouth shut and did my jobs like a good little servant. The last thing I needed was to make Kalani even madder than she already was.

I was just finishing vacuuming when the kids' mother came home. Mrs. Valdez took one look at me—now bedraggled in my dust-covered jeans and messy hair— and frowned.

"What are you supposed to be?" she asked. "I thought I hired a *princess* babysitting company."

"Oh. You did!" I exclaimed, reaching up to wipe the sweat from my brow. My heart pattered in my chest. "You totally did! It's just . . . something came up . . . and . . . Well, look! Kalani is all princessed out." I pointed to my friend. She scowled back at me.

"Yes," Mrs. Valdez agreed, "Kalani looks beautiful. She also got here on time. And she doesn't look like she just rolled out of bed." She shook her head. "You know, I gave you girls a chance because my daughters love princesses and I thought it would be a special treat. But if you can't even bother to dress up?" She frowned. "I don't think this is going to work out."

"I'm sorry!" I cried, horrified at what she was saying. After all, this was supposed to turn into a once-a-week job—we couldn't lose all that potential business because of my Sleeping Beauty snafu. "Look, I didn't mean to be late. It's just . . . I wasn't feeling well, and—"

"You're sick? You brought sickness into my house?" Mrs. Valdez cried, her expression going from angry to alarmed.

Uh-oh.

"Don't you understand? I cannot afford for Addison and Ava to get sick," she cried, looking truly panicked now. "If they get sick, I have to take off from work and . . ." She reached into her pocket and shoved a wad of bills in my face without bothering to count them. "Please just go."

I shook my head, feeling tears spring to the corners of my eyes. "That's okay. You don't have to pay me. And I'm sorry. I really am. I promise—I'm not the kind of sick that's contagious and—"

But she wasn't listening. She was diving under the kitchen sink, pulling out an economy-size bottle of bleach, presumably to sterilize anything and everything my germ-ridden, non-princessy hands might have touched. I sighed and headed out the door. Kalani joined me a moment later, looking almost as angry as Mrs. Valdez.

"How could you do that to me?" she demanded once we were back on the sidewalk. "I called you all afternoon and you didn't pick up the phone. Sarah offered to come over and help, but I told her you wouldn't just ditch me like that. That you *had* to be on your way."

"I'm sorry, Kalani! I fell asleep."

"If you were too tired, you could have let me know! I would have understood. But you just left me hanging. Without even a word!" Her voice cracked on the last part, and she looked like she wanted to cry too.

"I know! And I'm really, really sorry."

She shook her head. "Look, my parents think this is a terrible idea anyway. They are getting really annoyed with all the time this is starting to take. And I'm beginning to think they're right." She glanced back at the house we'd just exited. "Even Collin Prince is not worth this."

And with that she stormed away. I tried to call after her, but she refused to turn around. And so I was forced to watch her go, my stomach twisting into knots.

First Madison. Now Kalani.

This business was supposed to make all our dreams come true. So how come it was quickly turning into a nightmare?

22

SPEAKING OF NIGHTMARES, WHEN I FINALLY MADE IT HOME, my stepmother was sitting on the couch, waiting for me. I knew that was bad. Then I saw my dad's face on the iPad she'd propped up on the coffee table.

And I knew *that* was really bad.

"Hailey, your father and I need to talk to you," my stepmother said.

I glanced longingly at the stairs leading up to my cozy bedroom. All I wanted to do was collapse onto my bed and cry. Maybe even pass out and sleep till morning. But the looks on their faces told me I wasn't getting off the hook that easily. Not this time.

I slumped down onto a nearby armchair, avoiding

my stepmother's eyes. "Good to see you, too!" I muttered. "And why, yes, I did have a terrible day. Thanks for asking."

Out of the corner of my eye I caught my dad's scowl. "Sit up," he scolded. "This is serious, Hailey."

I grudgingly forced myself into a more upright position. "Sorry."

"Hailey, I got a call from school today. They said you weren't in attendance," my stepmother began.

"Yeah. Because you took off for work and left me without a ride. And your daughter refused to take me."

"Hailey, you know I can't be late when they call me to sub," she said. "And we spoke to Ginny already."

"Who told us you've been stealing her babysitting jobs?" my dad added. "Do you have any idea what she's talking about?"

Uh-oh.

"I didn't steal them!" I protested, my heart pounding uncomfortably in my chest. This was not good. "I just provided a superior service. It's called capitalism and . . ." I trailed off, trying to remember how Sarah had explained it.

My father and stepmother exchanged looks. "Hailey!

You and Ginny are not competing corporations. You are sisters," my father barked out from the iPad. "And as sisters you will treat each other with respect."

"Like she treats *me* with respect?" I cried. "Come on, Dad! She's like an evil stepsister from the movies. She treats me like I'm gum stuck to her shoe. What am I supposed to do? Kiss her butt? Do everything she says? Give away my hopes and dreams in order to help her fund her vast collection of patterned leggings?"

My stepmother looked troubled. I watched as she let out a long sigh, exchanging a look with my dad. I frowned.

"What?" I demanded.

"It's just . . . Ginny's going through a bit of a hard time right now," my stepmother said slowly. "I know that's no excuse for her bad behavior. But still. I need you to try to be understanding, okay?"

I frowned, surprised. Ginny was going through a hard time? Since when? The girl lived a blessed life, as far as I could see.

Suddenly her words from this morning came raging back to me.

You're not the only one in this family who needs money. . . .

"I don't understand," I said, against my better judgment. "What's going on with Ginny?"

But my stepmother only shook her head. "It's nothing that needs to concern you," she told me. "And everything will be just fine, I promise. Just . . . in the meantime, try to cut her some slack, okay?"

I slumped my shoulders. Of course they weren't going to tell me. It wasn't like I was a valued member of the family or anything. "Fine. Whatever. Can I go now?"

"No," my father said. "We have more to discuss."

I slumped back in my chair.

"Your history teacher sent me an e-mail," my stepmother said. "You failed a test yesterday. So I did some digging—called the rest of your teachers." She shook her head. "Hailey, you're barely passing any of your classes. And you haven't turned in completed homework in over two weeks."

My father scowled over the iPad, his voice rising in frustration. "Failing tests, skipping school—Hailey, this is not like you. Is this some sort of acting out because I'm gone? Because I really can't deal with this right now. I'm under a lot of pressure and . . ." He sighed.

I sat up in my seat, feeling guilty at the look I saw on his face. "Dad, I'm fine with you gone. I don't like it, but I get it, and this has nothing to do with that. I just . . . got behind, that's all. But I'm working to catch up. I'll talk to my teachers tomorrow, and I'll figure out a makeup test. And extra credit. Don't worry."

"Hailey, I'm afraid you're stretching yourself too thin," my stepmother interjected. "All these babysitting jobs. You're working practically every night. You are way too young to be doing that. Once in a while, sure. But I think it's time to take a break."

I stared at her, horrified. "No!" I cried. "I can't. Not now. Not when we're so close."

"Close to what? Going to a comic-book convention?" my father bellowed over FaceTime. "No." He shook his head. "Hailey, I don't care if these gigs would fund a trip to the moon. You will not flunk out of eighth grade."

I bit my lower lip. "Um, even for the moon? 'Cause I'm pretty sure the school board might give me a pass on that one . . ."

From across the world I could see my father's face redden, telling me I'd gone too far. "You are grounded, young lady. For the next week you are to come home right after school and start your homework immediately. No YouTube. No TV. No video games. And above all," he said, looking straight into my eyes, "no babysitting."

23

"OKAY," I SAID THE NEXT DAY AT LUNCH, "WE NEED TO DO some major rescheduling."

I explained the situation—that I was grounded for the next week. And how there were seven jobs that I wouldn't be able to cover.

"Can any of you help?" I asked.

"Not me," Madison said. "Playoffs are next week. Can't miss any more practices."

"And I'm not doing any more solo babysitting," Kalani added. "I learned my lesson on *that*." She gave me a pointed look. Clearly she was never going to let me forget my Sleeping Beauty snafu.

"Maybe you just need to cancel them," Sarah said.

"Call the parents and tell them something came up."

I sighed, staring down at the calendar. At all that potential money, just thrown away. "If I cancel this last minute, none of these people are ever going to hire us again. We'll be basically proving to them we're not dependable."

"No offense, Hailey, but we kind of are not dependable," Madison pointed out. "So they wouldn't be wrong."

"Maybe we just need to forget this whole thing," Sarah said. "We gave it our best shot. It just didn't work out."

"No!" I cried. "We can't give up now. Not when we've come so far!" I looked over at Madison. "How much money are we short at this point?"

She pulled up her phone, loading her calculator app. "With the money Kalani gave me this morning . . ." She pressed at the screen. "We're up to just under a thousand dollars."

"Which means we'd need at least six hundred more to make this work," Sarah pointed out before I could reply. "And that would be without eating or buying any souvenirs."

"I don't care about souvenirs," I said. "And I'd be

happy with a jar of peanut butter and a loaf of bread for the weekend."

"Sure. But that still leaves us six hundred short. Where are we going to get six hundred dollars in the next month?"

"Oh my gosh! Oh my gosh!" Kalani suddenly screeched, staring at her phone. We all turned to look at her, puzzled. "This is the best thing ever!"

"What?" I asked.

"Please tell me you've picked the winning Powerball numbers," Madison begged, "and are not just finding out they're serving pizza in the caf tomorrow."

"They're serving pizza in the caf tomorrow?"

Madison smacked her forehead with her hand. "Kalani!"

"Sorry." She looked down at her phone again then up at us. A grin stretched across her face. "My cousin just texted me. She's getting remarried!"

We groaned in unison. "So?" Sarah asked. Kalani's cousin, at last count, had been married three times and went through husbands like most people went through underwear.

"Seriously, how is that the best thing ever by any

stretch of the imagination?" Madison demanded.

"Because she needs someone to watch the kids at the wedding," Kalani explained. Her smile widened. "And . . . because it's a masquerade wedding—where everyone will be dressed up in costumes anyway—she wants to hire us to do it!"

I frowned. "Kalani, were you even listening to anything we just said? We can't take on any new jobs, remember?"

"I know. I know. But"—Kalani did a little happy wriggle dance in her seat—"she wants all four of us. For one night. And she's willing to pay . . . exactly . . ." She did a fake drumroll, by banging her hands against the table. "Six hundred dollars!"

We all stared at her, then at one another, dumbfounded. Six hundred dollars? Exactly six hundred dollars—the amount of money we needed to reach our goal? Six hundred dollars for just one night?

"When's the wedding?" I asked.

"Looks like in about two weeks. A Saturday night."

I nodded slowly. "I'll be off grounding by then."

"And the playoffs will be over," Madison added. "So I won't have practice or any games."

"And it's on a weekend," Sarah chimed in. "So my parents won't freak."

We fell silent for a moment, thinking it over. It almost sounded too good to be true. But there it was, right on Kalani's phone.

"Okay," I said. "I'll go and cancel the jobs we can't cover—the parents will just have to understand. And then we'll make this our very last job. We'll go to the wedding. Make the money. Then hang up our princess dresses for good."

My friends nodded slowly. Smiles spread across our faces.

"You know, Kalani," Madison said, "for once you may be right. This could very well be the best thing ever."

"And our very last chance," I declared, "for us to make our Collin Prince dreams come true."

24

TURNED OUT THERE WAS ONE UPSIDE TO BEING GROUNDED. IT
was really good for writing. Each evening, after I finished
my homework and presented it to Nancy for approval, I
would go back to my room and sit down at my computer
and get to work.

First I would work on my short story. Comicpalooza
was fast looming, and I needed to give Brody's dad time
to read it and give his comments. This way, if he had
any suggestions, I'd have time to work them in before
Comicpalooza.

Then, once I started getting bored of that and needed
a little inspiration, I'd go back to Collin Prince. Sarah
and I had been working on a brand-new story featuring

Collin as a valiant knight in shining armor and my best friend as a kick-butt dragon hunter, sent back in time to save the world. There was action, adventure, and, of course, because Sarah was the coauthor, romance. Bonus—it was turning out even better than I expected, and I found myself looking forward to getting home from school each day to work on it.

The other story was . . . less fun to work on. And certainly nothing I ever looked forward to writing. But I knew that real writing was not always fun and games— sometimes it was hard work. And serious writing had to be taken seriously. So I slogged away at it each day and forced myself not to delete every other sentence until I finally was able to type the very best sentence of all:

The end.

I stared at the words, a chill of pride winding up inside of me. It was finished—it was actually finished. A real story. Serious, literary, important with a capital *I*. My first real literature. Ready to take on the world.

Well, it would be once I got Brody's dad's notes. Hopefully he wouldn't have too many edits. After all, there wasn't a ton of time between now and Comic-palooza.

In any case, no time like the present to find out. And so, with hands shaking a bit from anticipation, I opened up my e-mail program and sent out two e-mails. One to Brody—with the short story attached. And the other to Sarah—with the next installment of the Collin Prince adventure.

E-mails sent, I leaned back in my chair, a small smile spreading across my face. I had done it. I had actually done it.

This definitely called for ice cream.

I had just finished eating the largest ice cream sundae known to mankind when my cell phone rang. I glanced at the caller ID, then grinned. It was Sarah. She must have gotten the chapter and read it already. I grabbed the phone, anticipating the excited screaming that was sure to be coming from the other end of the line. This was, after all, the best Collin Prince chapter yet. And the way I ended it? She'd probably already started the next part, just so she wouldn't be kept in suspense.

"So what did you think?" I asked, not bothering with saying hello. "Was it everything you ever dreamed of and more?"

"Um . . ." She sounded a little hesitant, which made me frown. "I don't get it."

"What?" I demanded, something uncomfortable stirring in my heart. Why wasn't she completely freaking out? Why wasn't she telling me I was the best friend ever? Did she not like the chapter? How could she possibly not like the chapter?

"Did you not like the chapter?" I blurted out.

"No. I did not, actually."

"What?" I pulled the phone away from my ear, staring down at it, confused as anything. "What are you talking about? How can you not like it? You love everything I write about Collin Prince."

"That's true. But the thing you sent me? It was not about Collin Prince," she snapped back.

Wait . . . what? Sarah was still talking, but I could no longer process her words.

"Hold on," I managed to squeak out, running to my computer to pull up my e-mail program and click on the sent folder, all the while my heart thudding uncomfortably against my chest. "Did I send you the wrong story?"

"What do you mean, wrong story?" Sarah's voice was

rising now. And it sounded angry. "There's more than one story?"

I couldn't answer. All I could do was stare at the screen as my stomach twisted into painful knots. In fact, it was all I could do not to throw up on the keyboard. I blinked my eyes a few times, praying that they were playing tricks on me. But the screen remained the same.

I had sent Sarah my Comicpalooza story.

Which meant I must have sent Brody . . .

"Oh no. No, no, no!" I cried.

"Hailey Smith. What is going on here? Why are you writing *other* stories when you're supposed to be working on one with me?"

"I am working on one with you. And I have the Collin Prince chapter, all ready to go. I just sent you the wrong one."

But Sarah clearly wasn't listening. "Is this the real reason you've been keeping me hanging every week?" she demanded. "You keep telling me you're so busy. That you don't have time to do the next chapter. Is that because you've been working on some other story instead?"

I drew in a breath, trying to stay calm, even as my pulse raced ice water through my veins. "Look, I just needed something to enter in the young writers' contest at Comicpalooza, that's all."

"Uh, you have something. *Our* story. Why not just enter that?"

"Come on, Sarah!" I ran a hand through my hair, exasperated. "That's just stupid fan fiction. This is an important award!"

Silence on the other end of the line. *Uh-oh.*

"Sorry," I amended. "I didn't mean it like that. I didn't mean—"

"That you think our story is stupid?" Sarah repeated back to me, her voice cold and quiet.

"Sarah . . ."

"I can't believe it. You've been lying to me this whole time. Telling me you have no time to write, all the while secretly spending that 'no time' on some superior contest-winning story that I'm evidently not good enough to help you with."

I squeezed my eyes shut and opened them again. "It wasn't like that," I protested. "I love writing with you. And I don't think our story is stupid. This was just something I started on the side. No one but Brody even knows about it."

I heard her suck in breath. "Brody. Of course. Selling out your best friend for a boy. Real nice, Hailey."

"I was going to tell everyone," I said weakly. "I was just waiting to see if I could really finish it first."

"Well, congratulations on finishing. I hope you win all the awards in the universe for this stellar, superior, not-stupid work of art. Just think—you already have Worst Best Friend Ever in the bag."

"Sarah!" I protested. But she had already hung up the phone.

I slumped back in my chair, my stomach churning. Why hadn't I just told her about the other story to begin with? Maybe then she wouldn't have been so mad. Of course she'd still want to enter the Collin Prince story in the contest. How could I explain to her how much that wouldn't work? That the editors were looking for real literature. Like the kind we read in English class in school. Not Collin Prince fan fiction. The kind I had just accidentally sent to Brody for his father to read.

Oh yeah. That.

I bounced back into action, grabbed my phone, and texted Brody. Maybe there was still time.

Sent wrong file–don't read! I'll send the real one now!

Sucking in a breath, I forced myself to go back to my computer and e-mail him the correct story this time. I e-mailed Sarah her chapter, too, along with a pleading apology, not that I thought she would read it at this point.

Tears stung my eyes as I picked up the phone to text Brody again. My fingers were shaking so hard I could barely type.

OK. New file sent.

Delete the old one.

Don't even open it. It's nothing.

It's just a grocery list. No big deal.

But delete anyway.

A moment later I got a text back.

Sorry. Already sent it to my dad. I'll send him the other file now.

I sank back in my chair. I was too late.

Please! Tell your dad not to read that story!

Uh, I thought you said it was a grocery list.

Yes! The grocery list! Don't let him read the grocery list!

I realized, vaguely, that I sounded like a crazy person. But I was feeling like a crazy person, so I guess that made sense. With a groan I threw my phone down onto my desk, wandered over to my bed, and collapsed onto the mattress. My eyes immediately went to the Collin Prince poster on my wall.

"Is it possible to die of humiliation?" I asked Collin. "Because I'm pretty sure I've got a critical case."

But Collin only smiled back at me without answering, the annoying way inanimate objects always do—outside cartoon films. I sighed, giving up and rolling over to grab my stuffed Charmander—who had always been my favorite Pokémon—and hugged it close, closing my eyes.

"It'll all be fine," I told myself. "Sarah will read the right chapter and forgive me, and Brody's dad will get the right story, and everything will be fine in the end."

Now if only I could make myself believe that to be true.

25

"SO TOMORROW'S THE BIG DAY!" I PRONOUNCED AS I SET MY tray down at the lunch table Friday afternoon. "The masquerade wedding. Our very last job—ever! Is everyone excited? Have you memorized your scripts? Sarah, did you get the masks from the theater department? Madison, did Brody give you the glow cube treasure?"

I stopped short as I realized Madison and Sarah were not looking at me. They were both staring down at their lunch trays, matching guilty expressions on their faces.

Uh-oh.

"What?" I demanded, my hands on my hips.

"Um, you know how it was raining last week?" Madison asked, still not looking at me. "And they canceled that playoff game?"

"Yeah . . ."

"Coach *just* told me they rescheduled it for tomorrow afternoon."

"Madison!"

"I'm sorry!" she cried, looking up at me. "I thought I'd be done by now! I was totally supposed to be, if it wasn't for that stupid rain." She sighed. "But I can't miss this, Hailey. The whole team is depending on me."

"I know. I know." I ran a hand through my hair, frustrated. "Okay. Fine. That stinks, but I'm sure we'll be able to manage without you. We'll still have three babysitters, after all."

"Um, actually, two babysitters," Sarah said, so quietly I almost didn't hear her.

"What?" I cried, jerking around to face her. She'd barely spoken to me since the whole Collin Prince story thing—but I didn't think she'd go as far as to let it affect the wedding gig and our trip to Comicpalooza.

She shrugged her shoulders, still not looking up at me. "My aunt is in the hospital," she muttered. "She's really sick. My mom wants to drive out early tomorrow morning to see her."

My heart went out to her. "I'm so sorry," I said. "I hope she's okay."

Sarah pushed back in her seat and stood up, then walked away without replying. I watched her go, sighing. While I was glad she wasn't bailing because of me, she was still bailing. I turned to Madison.

"I guess Kalani and I will have to handle it by ourselves, then."

"Handle what?" Kalani asked, dancing over to the table, late as per usual.

"Your cousin's wedding. Madison and Sarah can't make it." I bit my lower lip. "You're still planning to be there, right?"

"Duh!" Kalani declared. "I'm not going to miss my own cousin's wedding."

I let out a breath I hadn't realized I was holding. Okay. That was good. We would be fine. Sure, it wouldn't be easy—having only two of us to deal with the entire group of kids. But I had handled worse back at Bella's house my first day on the job. And Kalani and

I were both far more experienced now than we had been back then.

"What about Brody?" Madison asked. "Couldn't he pitch in?"

Kalani shook her head. "My cousin specifically asked for girl babysitters. I guess 'cause the bride and bridesmaids will be getting ready there, so they've made the inside of the house girls only until after the wedding."

"Right," I said. "Okay. We'll make it work. Can you meet after school and rework the scripts with me? So they work with two princesses instead of four?"

"Do you think the parents are going to be okay with that?" Kalani asked, looking a little worried. "I mean, what if they try to dock our pay because there's only two of us instead of four like they asked for? Like, they'd give us three hundred instead of six hundred or something."

I frowned. That *was* a possibility, wasn't it? And if we only made three hundred, well, we might as well not do the wedding at all. We needed six hundred minimum to make the Comicpalooza trip doable . . .

Suddenly an idea hit me. "What if they didn't know?"

My friends cocked their heads in confusion. "How would they not know?" Madison asked. "Even Kalani can count to four."

"Yeah, but we're not always going to be in the same place at the same time," I reminded her, as Kalani punched Madison in the arm. "And remember, it's a masquerade wedding. Meaning we'll all be wearing masks. Kalani and I can take turns being ourselves, then changing into your costumes and being you."

Madison and Kalani gave me matching doubtful looks. "You *really* think they're not going to notice?" Madison asked.

"Yes. They're at a wedding, remember? They're going to be crazy distracted and busy. As long as the kids are being cared for and kept out of their hair, they'll forget we're even there."

"I don't know . . . ," Kalani hedged. "It seems kind of deceitful. What if we get caught? No one will ever hire us again."

"Which is no problem," I reminded her, "since this is our last job anyway." I gave them a pleading look. "Come on, you guys! I don't know about you, but this Cinderella wants to go to the ball. And she doesn't have a fairy godmother to hook her up, so she's gotta take matters into her own hands. What was it you said, Madison? We princesses must save ourselves?"

She laughed. "I think I did say something like that."

"Well, then, consider this Operation Go to the Ball," I declared. "The final mission."

26

AFTER SCHOOL, KALANİ AND i MET UP AT A NEARBY TEX-MEX place to rework our scripts and plot world domination. By the time we headed home, we were both feeling pretty good about the whole thing. Sure, the costume changes would be a bit of a pain, but we'd make things easier on ourselves by wearing the smaller costumes under the bigger costumes and just ducking into the bathroom from time to time to put on them on—or take them off, as the case might be. And we could take turns doing it, so there would always be one person to watch the kids while the other was changing. It seemed like the perfect plan.

That night I forced myself to bed early. And I woke up in the morning ready to take on the world. Our final mission before retiring our tiaras for good. In a way, it was kind of bittersweet. It had been a lot of fun, princess babysitting, before things got so out of control. Maybe over the summer we could revive our business for a few jobs here and there—just for fun. With no pressure to make a certain amount of money in a limited time. And no conflicts with school and homework.

As I grabbed my dress and started to put it on, I heard a chime from my phone. It was a text from Brody.

Hey! My dad finally got a chance to read your story last night!

I swallowed hard, not sure how to respond, as my heart pounded in my chest. He'd read it. A real-life author had read my story. Now the question was, what did he think about it? Did he think it was worth entering in the contest?

Before I could reply, another text followed.

He said he really liked it and he had some thoughts to share with you. He's under major deadline for the next week, but could meet you after he turns his book in.

I squealed out loud, almost dropping the phone. *He liked it!* Oh my gosh, he'd actually read it and liked it! I could barely believe it! A real, live, published author had read my story and liked it! Now I could get his thoughts and edit the story and send it over to the Comicpalooza judges and . . .

Win all the awards in the universe for this stellar, superior, not-stupid work of art.

My happy smile faded as my mind flashed back to Sarah. To my stupidity on the phone with her almost two weeks ago now. As far as I knew she hadn't written a word since. And while she never said anything about it at school, I couldn't help but notice the hurt expression on her face, every time she looked at me. If she stopped writing altogether because of me . . . because I had made her feel like her work wasn't good enough . . .

I grimaced. Argh. I really was the world's worst best friend.

I glanced at the clock. I had an hour before I needed to get ready. Sitting down at my computer, I opened Microsoft Word. Then I placed my hands on the keyboard and started to type. A new chapter in the Collin Prince universe. Where a selfish, rotten girl learns a very valuable lesson about friendship—and undergoes terrible consequences for her bad behavior, losing her chance with Collin Prince forever. (Who ends up dating her super-cool, amazing, talented, sweet best friend instead—and falls in love forever.)

When I had finished, I uploaded it to Wattpad, where the rest of the story lived. I knew the website would send her a notification that it was there. I only hoped she'd go and read it.

In any case, now it was time to get ready. I pulled my beautiful princess dress out of the closet and gazed at it for a moment. This was the last time I'd ever wear it, I realized. The thought made me a little sad.

I'd just finished putting the last touches on my makeup when the doorbell rang. A moment later, Kalani stepped into my room.

"Here I am!" she said. Then she collapsed onto my bed.

I frowned, looking her over. "Is something wrong?"

She looked up, a little guiltily. "Why would anything be wrong?"

"No offense? But you're looking a little green."

"Oh." She gave a small shrug. "I'm not entirely sure those tacos last night agreed with me. But don't worry. I'll be—"

She stopped short. Her eyes widened into saucers. Suddenly she was pushing past me and running full speed out of my room and down the hall to the bathroom. A moment later my ears caught the worst sound in the history of sounds.

Full-on puking.

I sank down on my bed, my own stomach lurching. Oh no. Not now! Of all times—not now!

Kalani limped back into the room a few minutes later. "Um . . ." she said. "I was hoping I was done with all of that."

"With all of what? What do you mean? Was that not the first time you've thrown up?"

"Technically?" She winced. "It's the sixth time. I think, anyway. I kind of lost track at one point last night. I blame being delirious from the fever."

"You have a fever, too?" I fell back onto the bed, staring up at my ceiling. This was bad. This was really bad. "Were you even going to tell me?"

"No. Of course not! I mean, I wanted to. But I didn't want to let you down." Kalani gave me a desperate look. "Don't worry about it. I'll be fine. It only happens every hour or two and . . ." She trailed off. "Oh no," she said. Right before she puked all over her dress.

"Excuse me," she whimpered, and ran back to the bathroom.

I rose from my bed, pacing the room, my heart pounding at a desperate rate. There was no way I could bring her to the wedding like this. What if she got everyone sick? What if she puked on one of the guests? Or on a kid!

But what alternative did I have? If I didn't take her, then I'd be going solo. It was already going to be hard enough to play the part of two babysitters. Now I'd have to play all four? And I couldn't even cancel now—since we'd already lied about the other two. There was no way they were going to buy that three out of the four of us were suddenly stricken with the plague.

"Ew. It smells like puke in here."

I looked up to see Ginny hovering in the doorway. The last person I wanted to see. "What do you want?" I demanded.

"Nothing. Mom just wanted me to let you know lunch was ready."

"Thanks, but I'm not hungry."

She looked me over from head to toe. "You have a babysitting job today?" she sniffed. "I thought you were done with all that."

"We are," I said, not sure why I was even bothering to

explain. "We just have to do this one last wedding and—"

"So," Kalani interrupted, trouncing back into the room. Her dress was soaking wet from being washed and her makeup was all smudged. "That happened."

I sighed. "Kalani, go home and go back to bed," I told her. "I'll call you later."

"I can't go to bed! We've got the wedding in an hour!"

I could feel Ginny looking from one of us to the other, but I refused to dignify her questioning face with an answer. She'd love it too much—to know what a desperate situation we were in.

"It's fine. I'll take care of it. Now go get some rest. I'll call you later."

"No! Really, Hailey. I'll be—oh boy!"

I rolled my eyes as she ran out of the room again. Seriously, how much puke could one tiny girl's stomach contain? I'd have been impressed if I hadn't been so worried.

Ginny raised her eyebrows. "Looks to me like you're short a babysitter," she said.

"I'm short three babysitters, actually," I replied. "Thanks for noticing."

She paused for a moment, giving me a considering

look. Then she opened her mouth to speak. "Did you . . . need some help, then?" she asked. "I could probably find a dress somewhere. I think Mom has a few in her closet from when she was a bridesmaid. And I know I have a tiara somewhere in my room . . ."

I stared at her, surprised. Was she being serious? And if she was, should I take her up on her offer? After all, I was a bit desperate here. And beggars couldn't be choosers . . .

But in the end I shook my head. It just wouldn't work out. She didn't know the scripts or any of our games. And, most importantly, if I let her help, she'd want a share of the money. And we needed every last penny of that money for this to work.

"Thanks for offering," I said stiffly. "But I'll be fine."

She shrugged, gave me a look that could loosely be translated as *Your funeral*, and then exited my room. I watched her go, biting my lower lip, wondering if I'd made the right decision. Part of me wanted to call her back, to beg her to join me. Anything to not have to do this alone.

But no. This princess didn't need a fairy stepsister. She could do this herself.

At least I hoped I could. . . .

27

"HI! I'M HAILEY. REPORTING FOR BABYSITTING DUTY!"

The woman who answered the door looked behind me. "I thought there were going to be four of you," she said.

My knees wobbled a little, but I held my ground. "The other three are on their way. I just thought I'd get here a little early to meet everyone and get all the instructions I need for each kid. After all, you're going to be *so* busy later, I doubt you'll even have time to meet the other girls."

She laughed. "Good point." Then she held out her hand. "I'm Mrs. Wilding. I'm the mother of the bride. Katarina is really busy getting ready right now, so I hope you don't mind if we skip all the formalities of introduction."

I shook my head. I didn't mind one bit.

"Okay. Great." She stepped aside to allow me into the house. "Right now we have the girls in the playroom. We'll have you stay with them there until it's go time—to make sure they stay clean. Then you'll bring them outside for the ceremony. Once they do their flower girl thing, you'll bring them back here to change out of their dresses and into play clothes. Then they can run wild as far as I'm concerned." Her eyes locked on me. "Do you think you girls can handle that?"

"Oh yeah. Piece of cake," I declared, stepping into the playroom. Three adorable-looking redheaded triplet girls sat playing in the corner with their dolls. They looked a little like dolls themselves with their perfect curls and dimpled cheeks and pretty, lacy white dresses. When I said hello, they all looked up at me and gave me matching big smiles.

I smiled back. "Hello, girls," I said. "I'm Princess Awesome. And I am so excited to be here to play with you today."

They cheered and ran over to give me hugs. I hugged them back and patted each on the head. "We're going to have a great time!" I assured them. Then I turned to

Mrs. Wilding. "So wait. There are only three of them?"

She snorted. "*Only* three. Now that's a good one."

"Okay. So . . . no offense, but why did you hire four babysitters?"

"Well . . ." She glanced over at the triplets. "Let's just say they're not always on their best behavior. And it's *really* important to my daughter that nothing go wrong. So I figured why not? We're spending enough on this wedding as it is. Why not spend a little more . . . just in case?"

I nodded. "That's very smart," I said, though truth be told, it sounded a little idiotic to me. But hey—if she wanted to waste her money, who was I to say anything? I glanced over at the three girls, looking very relieved. Why, this wouldn't be bad at all! I could totally do this by myself.

"Okay," Mrs. Wildling said. "Then I'll leave you to your princessing." She smiled. "Great idea, by the way. The princess babysitting thing. I've told all my friends about it. They all want to meet you girls tonight." She grinned. "You may end the night with a *lot* of new customers!"

Uh-oh. Out loud, I said, "Um, that's great! But as you

know, our first priority will be the girls. So there may not be too much time for meet and greets."

She beamed at me. "See? I love you girls already." She glanced at her watch. "Oh my. I wanted to greet the others, but I must get back to my daughter. She's probably flipping out right now. Do you think you can handle it from here?"

"Absolutely. You go—check on your daughter. The girls and I will be fine."

Famous. Last. Words.

28

"OKAY, GiRLS!" I GREETED THE TRIPLETS WITH A BIG SMILE.
"Let's get this party started, shall we? Does everyone
have their masks?"

The three girls cheered, scrambling to grab their little
masks from a nearby table. I helped each of them attach
the mask to her face before putting on my own. I glanced
at my reflection in the mirror and smiled. It was perfect. No one would have any idea whether I was playing
myself—or one of my friends.

I turned back to the triplets, who were staring up at
me expectantly. I smiled. "Okay," I said. "We have a little time before the wedding. Who wants to see a magic
trick?" I sat down and reached into my bag to pull out

my Elsa wand. I'd do a little pretend snow to warm them up. Then maybe we could fly the teddy bear on the parachute. And then—

"I have to potty!" cried Triplet #1.

Of course she did. I sighed. "Okay," I said. "Well, then we'll start off by playing Go to the Potty!" I rose to my feet and clapped my hands. "Everyone ready?"

Triplets #2 and #3 frowned. "We don't want to go to the potty," said Triplet #2.

"We want to stay here and play," said Triplet #3, crossing her pudgy arms across her chest.

I glanced out of the playroom, biting my lower lip. This was where having at least one backup would have come in handy. But the bathroom was just across the hall—I could see it from here. Surely the other two girls could play by themselves for a few minutes while I took their sister to pee. After all, they'd been playing nicely by themselves before I got here.

"Okay," I said. "But stay right here. Do not leave this room."

"Yes, Princess Awesome."

I let out a breath of relief. Then I led Triplet #1 to the bathroom and helped her inside. It was a very small powder room, and I barely fit with my dress.

"Are you sure you can't do this by yourself?" I asked the little girl.

"I need to poop," she said proudly. "I need you to wipe me when I poop."

Awesome.

I glanced at the door, which I'd left open a crack, to try to keep an eye out for the other two girls. I could hear them giggling from across the hall.

"Okay, fine," I said. "But hurry up, okay? I don't want to leave your sisters for too long."

She gave me a skeptical look. "You can't rush a poop, Princess Awesome."

Right. Silly me.

From across the hall I heard a loud crash. I winced. *Uh-oh.*

"Um, you go ahead and start . . . doing your thing," I told the little girl. "I'm just going to go check on your sisters. I'll be back in a second to wipe you."

"Okay."

I pushed through the door and dashed across the hall, back into the playroom. Triplet #2 looked up at me with a proud grin. In the approximately three seconds I'd been away, she'd somehow managed to trash the entire playroom—including pulling off every single book from a huge bookcase onto the floor. It would have been impressive had it not been so horrifying.

"What did you do?" I cried.

She shrugged. "I wanted something to read."

This might have been a believable answer, I supposed, if she had been holding an actual book. Instead she was sitting across the room, playing with two Barbie dolls.

It was then that I realized the bigger problem. "Where's your sister?" I demanded, praying she wasn't actually buried under the huge pile of heavy books.

"She went to find you," Triplet #2 said, matter-of-factly. "She said she had to pee too."

Ugh. I ran a hand through my hair, frustrated. "Okay. You pick up those books. I'm going to find your sister. Do not leave the room."

"Yes, Princess Awesome."

"Princess Awesome! I need to be wiped!" came from across the hall.

Perfect. "I'll be right there!"

I gave Triplet #2 a warning look, then ran across

the hall to the bathroom. But before I could squeeze back inside, an elderly woman with large, thick glasses stepped into my path. She peered at me quizzically, squinting her eyes.

"Are you . . . no. You're not Kalani," she said. "Are you?"

"Um. No. I'm Hailey. You, uh, know Kalani?"

"Yes!" The woman beamed. "I'm her great-aunt. I heard she would be here today, helping with the babysitting, and I'd love to see her. It's been so long!" She peered behind me. "Is she . . . here?"

I swallowed hard. Duh. It was Kalani's cousin getting married—it made sense she'd have relatives in attendance. "She's . . . here," I blurted out, not knowing what else to say. "Um, but I think she's off helping one of the triplets to the bathroom. And she'll, uh, be right back!"

"Great! I'll wait for her, then."

"Uh, you really don't . . . I could have her find you . . . I mean, when she . . ."

But Kalani's aunt was already pushing past me and heading into the playroom. Great. I swallowed hard, my heart pounding nervously in my chest. I should have told her Kalani wasn't here yet. Or something. Anything.

"Princess Awesome! I need to wipe!"

Right. I dashed back into the bathroom, grabbing a huge swatch of toilet paper in the process. I did the deed, then shooed the triplet back into the playroom. Kalani's aunt looked up at me. "Did you find her?"

"Um." I tried to give her a bright smile, but probably came off looking like a crazy person. Thank goodness she was obviously very nearsighted. "Not yet. But I will." I paused, then added, "Can you watch these two girls for a second while I do?"

"Of course!" she cried. "I would love to! Such sweet girls!"

I let out a breath of relief. "Okay. Be right back."

I raced down the hall, my gaze darting from left to right, desperate to find my missing charge. As I turned the corner and entered the kitchen, I found her, digging her grubby little fingers into the wedding cake. No!

"What are you doing?" I demanded, grabbing her and yanking her away.

"I was hungry!" she cried, bursting into tears.

"You can eat later!" I frantically brushed the crumbs (a.k.a. evidence) from her dress, then grabbed a knife to smooth over the finger hole in the cake best I could.

Then I grabbed her hand and pulled her from the kitchen. "Come on!"

We headed back toward the playroom. Halfway there I remembered that Kalani's aunt was still waiting. So I pulled the little girl into the bathroom with me and shut the door.

"What are we doing?" she demanded.

"Your sister said you had to pee," I told her, as I pulled off my top dress for a quick changeroo, faster than Superman in a phone booth. Underneath I was wearing Madison's short pirate princess dress. Not exactly something Kalani would have worn, but her great-aunt wouldn't know that.

"Why are you changing?" Triplet #3 demanded, giving me a suspicious look.

"Don't you change *your* princess costumes?" I shot back.

She considered this for a moment. "Yes," she said at last. "Once I was even Elsa *and* Cinderella at the same time." She looked pleased with herself.

"That must have looked really cool," I told her, pulling my hair back into a bun. My hair wasn't as dark as Kalani's, but hopefully pulled back that wouldn't be noticeable, especially to a nearsighted aunt. "Right now, I am playing Princess Kalani." I ushered her out of the bathroom. "Princess *Kalani*. You got that? Now let's go find your sisters."

We stepped back into the playroom. My eyes widened in horror as I found Kalani's aunt, tied up to the rocking chair she'd been sitting in. To make matters worse, there were no triplets to be seen.

"Oh my gosh. What happened?" I cried. "Um . . . Auntie?" I added, remembering I was supposed to be playing the part of my friend. Not that I was sure it mattered much at this point.

"Oh, nothing! The girls wanted to play hide-and-seek," the aunt said brightly. "I had to be tied up first. So I didn't cheat." She giggled. I stifled a groan of frustration.

"So where are they now?"

"Oh, I don't know, my dear. I wasn't paying attention." She beamed up at me. "Kalani, did you dye your hair?"

"Um, yes?" I dropped to my knees and struggled with her ropes. Who knew a couple of four-year-olds could tie knots like a sailor? It took me nearly a minute to get her free.

And when I finally did? Triplet #3 had left the building. Argh!

"Gotta go," I said, running out of the room. I could hear Kalani's aunt calling out to me, wanting to know how school was and if I was doing my homework, but I ignored her, trying desperately to locate my three missing charges. I checked the bathroom first, then headed back to the kitchen, to see if they'd attacked the cake again. As I ran around the corner, I almost dove headfirst into Mrs. Wilding herself.

"Oh! Hello!" she said. "You must be one of the other babysitters. I met your friend—Hailey, was it?—earlier."

"Yes. I'm . . . um, Madison," I said, trying to catch my breath. "Um, have you seen the girls around? I think they're with Sarah. Or Madison—I mean, Hailey!" I barked out a laugh. "'Cause obviously *I'm* Madison. So I would know if they were with me. . . ."

Mrs. Wilding frowned at me. "Is something wrong?" she asked.

"Oh no!" I cried in my most cheerful *of course nothing's wrong* voice. "We were just playing . . . hide-and-seek to pass the time."

Mrs. Wilding glanced at her watch. "Okay. Well, now

might be the time to start rounding them up and calming them down. We've got thirty minutes to showtime, and I really need them to keep their dresses clean."

"Not a problem," I assured her.

This was a problem.

I raced to the kitchen, then into the living room. No triplets to be seen. My breath was now coming in ragged gasps, and my heart was pretty much in my throat. Where were they? How could all three of them just disappear? It wasn't *that* big a house.

I found a set of stairs and dashed up them, discovering a game room and media room at the top. A few women were hanging out inside, chatting with one another. I tried to slip into the room, unnoticed, peering around for any sight of something triplet shaped.

"Look!" cried one of the women on the couch. "It's one of the princess babysitters!"

Everyone turned to look at me. *Uh oh.*

"Um, hi?" I said, my eyes darting around the room, but coming up empty. Where were they? Did they have some kind of cloak of invisibility or something?

"Isn't she adorable?" cried another woman. "What's your name, honey?"

"Um. Sarah. My name is Sarah. It's nice to meet you. Now I really have to—"

"You must tell us all about your little babysitting business. Such a great idea. I have two children myself, you see. And I'm always looking for good, reliable babysitters."

"Well, then you're not looking for us," I muttered.

"Excuse me?"

"Sorry. Nothing. I'm . . . I'll have to give you our flyer later. Right now I have to . . ."

I trailed off, my ears catching what sounded like a small giggle.

"Excuse me," I said, dashing out of the room. As I did, I caught a flash of red just around the corner. I ran after it. If I could at least get one of them . . .

Suddenly I was flying through the air, then slamming down hard onto the floor. My ankle jammed, and I yelped in pain. When I glanced behind me, I realized I'd been tripped by a tricycle. (Who kept a tricycle inside, anyway?)

The good news: Two of the triplets were standing above me.

The bad news: I could no longer stand at all.

"Where's your sister?" I asked, trying to get up. My ankle protested with another sharp pain.

"We'll go get her!" they cried, running in the other direction.

"No! Wait!" I begged. But they were already gone. And this time I couldn't run after them.

Somehow I managed to get to my feet. As I limped past the media room, I heard a voice from inside. "Hey! Can you come back here? I want to hear about the princess babysitting."

"Trust me, you really don't," I mumbled under my breath.

Tears pricked my eyes as I tried to make my way down the stairs and back toward the playroom, praying that the triplets had all returned there on their own. But of course I wasn't that lucky. And when I entered the room, there was no sign of them.

I collapsed onto the rocking chair, my head in my hands. What was I going to do? There was no way I could round up all three of them, not with my ankle. And the wedding was fast approaching. Why had I thought I could do this by myself? And now what was I supposed to do? Mrs. Wildling would realize I'd lied. She'd flip out.

Maybe she'd even call the police! Could I get arrested for lying? Child endangerment, maybe?

As if on cue, Mrs. Wilding poked her head into the room. "Where are the children?" she demanded. "My daughter wants to see them before the ceremony begins." She looked around the room, a frown etched across her face. "And where are the other babysitters? Are there only two of you? I've only seen two of you. . . ."

"It's fine," I said, giving one last, hopefully confident-looking smile. "Everything's fine. I'll go get the girls. And we'll head over to see the bride."

She nodded, still looking a little suspicious, but thankfully, she didn't try to press me—and instead headed back out the door. As her footsteps faded into the distance, I sucked in a breath, my heart beating out of control. Sweat poured down my face. My ankle throbbed in protest. What was I going to do? I was officially out of options.

Except . . . I lifted my head. Maybe one . . .

29

"OKAY. WE'RE HERE. HOW CAN WE HELP?"

I had to admit, Ginny and Jordan looked a little like fairy godmothers as they swept into the playroom, dressed in their mothers' bridesmaids' gowns, complete with lots of costume jewelry and tiaras on their heads. It was actually impressive costuming—especially on such short notice. I let out a sigh of relief, feeling the tears prick at the corners of my eyes. I wanted to hug them both—but decided that might end up being a bit awkward.

Instead I rose to my feet. My ankle was feeling a little better, but it still hurt to put my full weight on it. "The wedding starts in ten minutes," I told them. "And the triplets are running wild around the house somewhere. We need to wrangle all three of them together and drag them out onto the back lawn, where the ceremony is taking place."

"Okay. We're on it." Ginny gave Jordan a brisk nod. "Divide and conquer."

I watched them exit the playroom, feeling weak with relief. Thank goodness my stepsister had answered the phone and had been willing to help. I had been completely out of other options.

Of course I'd had to promise her half my take-home pay—meaning the dream of going to Comicpalooza was over forever. But at that moment I would have gladly handed over my entire life's savings for an extra pair of hands and legs.

I limped though the house, searching everywhere for the triplets. In closets, under the stairs, around corners. I was almost ready to give up, in fact, when I finally found Triplet #1 in the shower stall of her mother's bathroom. But just as I was about to sigh in relief, I caught a glimpse of her face and gasped.

"Do I look pretty?" she asked brightly.

I staggered backward, horror washing over me. My

eyes darted around the trashed bathroom—and then back to her white dress. Which was not very white anymore. In fact, it was covered in glitter. She must have dumped an entire bowl of the stuff on her head. She'd also attacked her mother's makeup, from the looks of it. Smudged red lipstick, slashed across her entire face. Garish blue eyeshadow—repurposed as blush.

I moaned, dropping to my knees in front of her, trying to brush it off. But it was no use. She'd gotten wet in the shower, and the glitter was stuck fast. It would take washing the entire dress to get it out. And we didn't have time for that.

"Come on," I said, dragging her out of the bathroom and back down the stairs. To my relief I found Ginny and Jordan at the bottom, each with a triplet by the scruff of the neck. Their eyes widened as they saw my charge.

"Holy pixie dust!" Ginny said with a low whistle.

"I look pretty!" protested the triplet. "Don't I look pretty?"

I groaned. "I was supposed to keep them clean," I confessed to my stepsister and her friend. "That was my one job! To keep them looking pristine until after the ceremony. What am I going to do? The wedding starts in, like, five minutes."

Ginny and Jordan exchanged looks. "Well . . . she doesn't look bad," Jordan said. "The glitter is kind of pretty, actually. If you wiped all that makeup off her face."

"Yeah, but they don't match . . . ," I started to say. Then I stopped, looking at my stepsister. She grinned, telling me she was thinking the exact same thing I was.

"I don't know," I hedged. "What if they don't like it? They could be really annoyed."

"Or they could be really impressed—if we do it right," Ginny replied. She turned to Jordan. "Go find that glitter and meet me in the playroom. I've got an idea."

Jordan ran up the stairs. Ginny beckoned for me to follow. "Okay, kids, let's go." She turned to the little girls. "And no more running off," she scolded. "Or you'll go to time-out and miss your mommy's wedding."

The girls stared at her, horrified. Then, to my surprise, they fell into line behind her, the little devils, suddenly walking like angels on their way to church.

"How did you do that?" I whispered to Ginny as we headed down the hall.

She shrugged. "It becomes easy after a while. The

basic rule? You have to earn their respect. Remember, you're not here on a play date. Your number one job is to keep them safe—not entertained. You may look like a princess. But you have to act like the queen. And the queen's word is law."

I nodded, considering this. That was actually pretty wise. Ginny and Jordan might be boring babysitters, but that didn't mean they weren't good.

We arrived back at the playroom and Ginny proceeded to rummage through a large chest of costumes I hadn't noticed before until she found and pulled out three sets of fairy wings. She turned to the triplets, holding them up in her hands.

"If you're going to be covered in pixie dust," she said, "you might as well look like actual pixies."

The girls' eyes lit up like it was Christmas morning. Without hesitation they dove for the wings. Laughing, I helped Ginny affix a set on each girl, though deep down I still wondered if we were overstepping our bounds. After all, if the bride had wanted wings, wouldn't she have asked for wings? But then, she hadn't asked for them to be covered in glitter, either. Desperate times and all that.

A moment later, Jordan returned. "There isn't a ton

left," she said. "But I think we can make it work." She put her fingers to her mouth and blew loudly, getting the triplets' attention. "Line up!" she commanded. "And let's do this."

One by one Jordan glittered up Triplet #2 and #3 until they all matched, while Ginny worked to wipe the makeup off Triplet #1's face. When they were finished, they lined up for inspection. I had to admit, as a trio, they looked pretty cute. And, more important, they looked intentionally sparkly, instead of like the *I escaped my babysitter and raided my mother's makeup* variety.

"Okay," I said, my heart still pumping madly in my chest. I glanced at my watch. "I think it's time to go outside. Come on, girls. Let's do this."

As we stepped outside, as if on cue the music started to play. We led the girls down to the back of the aisle, where an usher handed each of them a basket of flowers. They giggled and, when prompted, pranced down the aisle, tossing the flowers around, as if they were born to do the job, while everyone clapped and cooed about how cute they looked and how the wings and glitter were such a special touch.

I glanced over at Ginny and Jordan. They grinned

at me, and Ginny gave me a discreet thumbs-up before turning back to the ceremony.

I let out a sigh of relief, a small smile creeping across my face. I couldn't believe it. We had pulled it off. And by doing so, I had learned a very valuable lesson: that while a princess should always try to save herself, it could never hurt to have a few friends on call.

And maybe evil stepsisters weren't always evil after all.

30

"THANK YOU GIRLS SO MUCH!" CRIED MRS. WILDING MUCH later, after the triplets had gone to bed and the wedding was winding down. "You did a fabulous job. And the fairy thing! Well, I can't even tell you how many people came up to me to tell me how cute they were. Who would have ever thought to add glitter and wings?" She grinned. "In fact, the photographer told me he was going to upload a few of the photos to Pinterest to show off the idea to other brides."

I grinned. "That's great!" I said. "I'm so glad it worked out. And, um, I'm sorry Kalani had to leave early before you got to say hi. She just wasn't feeling a hundred percent and didn't want to get anyone infected." (Which wasn't technically a lie, right?)

"Oh, that's okay." Mrs. Wilding waved a hand. "Her great-aunt told me she saw her earlier and that she seemed a little off. Poor thing." She shook her head. "In any case, I suppose I should pay you now so you can get on your way." She rummaged in her bag, then pulled out a wad of bills. "I know I promised you six hundred, right? But here's seven hundred—you more than earned your keep. After all, I know how those girls can be. They look angelic, but . . ."

"They *were* angelic," I assured her. "But thank you. We had a lot of fun with them." I took the money and put it in my pocket. Then I turned to Ginny and Jordan. "I guess we should head out," I said.

"Do you need a ride?" Mrs. Wilding asked.

"Nah. I have a car," Ginny assured her. "But thank you anyway."

I had a fleeting worry, as we walked outside, that Ginny would revert back to evil-stepsister mode and refuse to drive me home, but she opened the car door and gestured for me to get in. Once we were all inside the car, I reached into my pocket and counted out the money.

"Thank you, guys," I said. "You saved my life."

"We were happy to make the money," Ginny assured

me. "Let's just say business hasn't exactly been booming lately, if you know what I mean."

I groaned, handing over her share. "Well, it should pick up soon," I assured her. "This was it for us. We're hanging up our tiaras for good." Then I reached back into my pocket. "And here. I'm going to give each of you three hundred. You more than deserve it."

Ginny frowned. "Are you sure, Hailey? Don't you need the money?"

I waved her off. "If it weren't for you saving my butt, I wouldn't have gotten paid at all."

"Actually, I think we made a pretty good team," Jordan declared, plucking the bills from my hand and stuffing them into her pocket. "Now. How about we go spend some of this windfall on pancakes? I know a twenty-four-hour diner. . . ."

We stuffed ourselves with pancakes until we could barely move, then dropped Jordan off at her house before heading home for the night. When we walked in together, laughing and reminiscing about the glitter, my step-mother raised her eyebrows.

"Why are you two acting so chummy?" she asked

suspiciously. "Did pigs learn to fly while I was at my book club?"

"Nah," I said, blushing a little. "Just turns out my wicked stepsister is actually pretty cool."

Ginny made a mock protest. "Hang on! I thought you were the wicked one!"

I laughed, then turned serious. "Well, maybe I *have* been a bit wicked," I admitted. I turned to my stepmother. "I'm sorry I've been such a jerk lately," I said. "To both of you."

My stepmother's eyes softened. "Come here," she beckoned. I took a step forward, and she drew me into her arms, giving me a warm hug. Then she pulled away, meeting my eyes with her own. "I know it's not easy for you," she said. "Having your dad so far away. It's not easy for me, either."

"Yeah. I know. You didn't ask to be stuck with me."

She chuckled. "For the record? I happen to *like* being stuck with you," she told me. "And you may not believe this, but I actually don't like being the wicked stepmother all the time. If it were up to me, we'd just be friends. But . . ." She trailed off, sighing.

I looked at her. My mind suddenly flashed back

to the triplets running wild through the house. How Ginny and Jordan had effortlessly brought them back into line.

You may look like a princess. But you have to act like a queen.

"You're not a wicked stepmother," I assured her. "In fact, as far as stepmothers go? You're pretty great."

"Well, you're a pretty great stepdaughter yourself," she said, tears welling in her eyes. She pulled me back into her arms, practically crushing me in another hug.

"Hey, don't forget me!" Ginny cried, throwing herself into the hug with such enthusiasm we lost our balance and fell onto the couch, laughing.

After untangling herself, my stepmother gazed at us with fond, watery eyes. "My girls," she said. Then she headed upstairs.

Once she was gone, I turned to my stepsister. "Thanks again for helping me tonight," I said. "I know I didn't deserve you to."

"No big deal. Plus, I was glad to make the money."

"What *do* you need the money for, anyway?" I asked, curious. "I'm guessing now it isn't for a new pair of patterned leggings."

She smiled. "While I am always up for a new pair of leggings," she assured me, "I'm actually trying to save for college."

"Wait. I thought your dad was paying for that."

The smile fell from her face. She kicked the floor with the toe of her shoe. "Yeah. Me too," she said quietly. "But he lost his job a couple months ago. And he had to empty the college account to pay his rent or whatever." She made a face. "So I guess it's now up to me. I've got two years to save all I can."

I swallowed hard, not sure what to say. All this time I'd been gleefully stealing her babysitting jobs just so I could meet some YouTube star, while she was actually trying to save for her future. My stomach lurched, and suddenly I felt a little sick.

"Why didn't you tell me? If I had known . . ."

She turned away, staring at the wall. "I guess I was . . . embarrassed?" she finally said. "I mean, your dad? He's so great. He's living in a hotel room across the world just so he can provide for us. And we're not even his real family."

Her voice cracked and my heart broke. I crossed the room, pulling her into a hug. "You are real family," I told her sternly. "And I'm very glad you're my sister."

"I'm glad you're mine, too," she said. Then she laughed. "Even if you are a better babysitter."

I shook my head. "Trust me—I am *so* not a better babysitter. I've just got a cool wardrobe. Which you're welcome to borrow," I added. "Since as of today Princesses and Pirates, Incorporated, is officially looking for new ownership." I grinned. "*If* you happen to know someone who might be interested in making a lot of money this summer . . ."

Ginny's eyes widened. "Really? You'd let me take over the business?"

"If the shoe fits . . . it's all yours."

31

"OKAY, LADIES. THE COLLIN PRINCE FAN CLUB SESSION HAS now come to order."

Madison rapped her gavel onto my bedpost. We were meeting at my house, the day after the wedding, as her mother was working on yet another remodel project for some sort of magazine photo shoot. Madison swore her mother changed her house around so many times—one day she'd get lost coming home, not recognizing it.

"The Collin Prince funeral session, you mean," Kalani said mournfully. She poked her stomach. "Thanks to you, you dumb, taco-hating belly."

Madison gave me a rueful look. "Sorry, Hailey. I know we all let you down."

"It's okay," I said. "We gave it our best try. And it's not like we didn't make money. We should try to find something fun to do with it. Or maybe just save it for now," I added, thinking of Ginny and her college fund. You never knew when hard times could hit, and it couldn't hurt to have a little extra stashed away, just in case.

"What are we going to do with the dresses?" Sarah asked. "'Cause mine is taking up a lot of closet space."

"Maybe we could sell them back to the thrift store?" Kalani suggested. "We could get credit to buy some more practical stuff we might actually wear again."

I glanced over at my closet. At my dress, which still hung from a hanger on the door. My heart squeezed a little. It was so beautiful, even if it was a little impractical. (Okay, fine, a lot impractical.) The idea of getting rid of it made me sad. But what else were we supposed to do with them? It wasn't like we'd ever have an opportunity to wear them. And they would just end up gathering dust and taking up room.

"I guess you're right," I said after a pause. I offered them to Ginny since they're taking over the business, but she said they'd get their own. "I can see if my stepmother can drive us to the thrift store later today."

"Thrift store?"

We looked up to see that Nancy had stepped into the room. She smiled at us. "Sorry to intrude," she said. "I just thought you girls might be hungry." She held out a plate of cookies, which we eagerly grabbed. After taking a bite and swallowing it, I turned to my stepmother.

"Can you drive us to the thrift shop today?" I asked. "We need to sell our princess dresses."

"So you're done for good, then?" she asked. "You're sure?"

I nodded. "Yeah. I gave all our families to Ginny and Jordan. They're going to take over the business and create their own costumes. We've got way too much other stuff going on."

She looked us over, nodding slowly. "Understood," she said. "Though I did have one thought. . . ."

I cocked my head in question. "What is it?"

"The St. Francis Group I've been volunteering for is starting a new initiative. They want to bring in special guests and performers to local hospitals to entertain young cancer patients. I thought it might be perfect for you guys."

My heart rose in my chest. "Really? We could perform at the hospital?"

"Don't get too excited," my stepmother interrupted. "It's not like a babysitting job or a wedding. It's for charity—so you wouldn't get paid."

Oh. Our heads sank. Of course.

"But," she added, "I'm sure the kids would *really* appreciate it. They don't have much to look forward to in their lives. It would probably mean a lot." She shrugged. "Anyway, no pressure. I just thought I'd let you know of the opportunity. No big deal either way."

And with that she scooped up the empty cookie plate and headed out of the room, closing the door behind her. I watched her go, then turned back to my friends.

"I really thought for a second she was going to say it was a real job," Sarah said, looking dejected.

"Yeah. Like there was actually a chance still—to get the money for Comicpalooza," added Madison.

Kalani sighed. "We have to face facts. There is literally no way that's going to happen now."

"Right." I bit my lower lip. "Still. I think we should do this anyway."

The girls looked up at me. "What? Why?" Madison asked.

I shrugged. "Remember when we started this whole

thing? How fun it was? Dressing up as princesses, working on our scripts, playing with the kids. I know it was all for money . . . but it was also kind of great, right?"

I smiled, remembering that first day with Brody and the crazy random pirate treasure. "We started this business together," I reminded them. "And we were supposed to do our last job together too, but that didn't work out. So what about this? What about putting on the dresses just one more time? Not for money. But for the kids. *And* our friendship."

Everyone nodded their heads in agreement. We were going to do this . . . once more with feeling.

And speaking of friendship . . .

Sarah turned to me. "Can I talk to you for a second?"

I somehow managed to nod, my heart in my throat. I followed her out of the bedroom and into the living room, settling down next to her on the couch. I watched as she stared down at her hands, as if gathering courage to talk. I wanted to say something. But I knew it was better to wait for her to say what she wanted to say.

She drew in a breath. "I had a lot of time to kill while at the hospital," she said. "And I read your story."

I nodded. "Okay."

"It was . . . funny," she said, a small, reluctant smile playing at the corners of her lips. "Really funny. You're a good writer, Hailey."

"You're a good writer too," I said quietly. "I'm sorry if I made it seem like I didn't think so. Trust me—it wasn't that at all. It's just . . . you were so excited to be doing the Collin Prince story, and I didn't want to let you down."

"I would have understood, you know," she said. "I mean, I know you want to be a writer, and I would have totally cheered you on at the contest."

"I know you would have. And I'm sorry." I gave her a rueful look. "Also, for the record, I love our Collin Prince story. And I don't want to stop working on it . . . with you."

She looked up at me for the first time, her eyes shining. "Really?" she asked.

"Really."

She grinned. "I was hoping you'd say that." She reached into her bag and pulled out a stack of papers. "Because I wrote the next chapter this morning," she informed me, plopping the papers on my lap. "So it's your turn again."

"Awesome," I said. "I'll get started on it right now."

32

"OKAY, MY FIERCE AND NOBLE PRINCESSES AND PIRATES! WE
are finally here. We stand at the doorway to the great
temple, where treasure has been hidden for a thousand
years. We have fought long and hard to get here, and now
it will be ours." I turned to the kids who stood behind
me, dressed in their princess and pirate best, their eyes
shining with excitement. "Get behind me now. For I am
about to unleash my magic. Are you ready?"

"Ready!" the kids chimed, scurrying into position
with a little help from Sarah, my princess assistant.
Smiling at her, I readied my wand.

"Okay. On the count of three . . . One . . . two . . ."

"Who dares disturb my treasure trove?"

Madison burst into the room in full pirate regalia, Kalani and Brody dancing by her side. The kids screamed, ducking behind me. Madison shot me a quick grin before getting back into character. "You think you can just walk right in here and steal my treasure, do you?" she demanded, strutting up and down the hospital playroom, giving an evil eye to each kid in turn. They giggled and squealed, their faces flush with excitement. "Well, the way I see it, every last one of you will be walkin' the plank before the night is through!"

"Um, literally!" Kalani chimed in, evidently forgetting her lines. But everyone laughed, so I guess that was okay.

"Nay!" cried Sarah, stepping up beside me. "It will be *you*, evil pirates, who will be defeated tonight. By me and my valiant group of princess and pirate warriors."

She turned to our group, clapping her hands together. "Are you ready?" she asked.

"Ready!" they cried.

"On the count of three, I want you to use your warrior ninja magic and *push* the pirates away. One, two . . . *three!*"

She waved her arms in the air. The kids followed suit,

mimicking the Jedi-like moves we'd taught them earlier. Brody gasped, his hand going to his throat. He stumbled to the floor, Kalani following suit. Madison turned to the kids, a horrified look on her face.

"No!" she cried. "Not the ninja magic! Anything but the ninja magic!"

I stepped up to the two of them. "Do you seek mercy? Are you sorry for your evil ways?"

"We're sorry!" Kalani cried. "Please, mighty princess. Free us from the ninja magic and we will be good pirates from now on."

I turned to the kids. "What do you think? Should we believe them?"

"No!" the kids cried.

I laughed, turning back to our pirates, who were still struggling for breath. "Sorry, guys. My squad has decided. It's Davey's Locker for you."

I waved my hands, flicking my wand in the direction of the evil pirates. They screamed and froze into statues—defeated by my all-powerful magic.

I turned back to the kids and smiled. They all cheered. I took a little bow, then walked over to a corner, where I had stashed the loot.

"You have done well, my princesses and pirates," I told them. "And now we shall share in the treasure." With a flourish, I swept open the chest. The kids squealed in excitement at all the prizes inside. Glow cubes, little toys, shiny golden coins, plastic tiaras. We had hit up Party City hard before coming here—thanks to my stepmother's donation to the cause—and created our best and biggest loot stash yet.

As the kids rummaged happily through the box, taking all the prizes they wanted, I turned to my friends, a big grin on my face. This had been our best show ever. And, even better: For the first time, we'd gotten to do it together as a group.

I settled into my seat, watching the kids, a warmth washing over me, even as my heart squeezed a little. In anticipation of our coming, they'd all dressed as princesses or pirates, with sparkling costumes of every color, donated by my stepmother's charity group. A local wig company had also provided beautiful long-haired wigs for the occasion, since most of the kids had lost their real hair to chemotherapy, and the little girls wore them with pride, topped with tiaras.

But all the costumes in the word couldn't compete

with their faces—which were practically glowing with happiness. Except . . .

I frowned. My eyes settled on one little girl sitting alone in the corner, her knees pulled up to her chest. She looked about six years old and stood out from the rest of the group, the only one not wearing a wig or costume. She looked extremely unhappy, watching from the sidelines but refusing to participate in the treasure grab.

"Who is she?" I asked a nearby nurse. "Doesn't she want to join the others?"

"Oh." The nurse gave me a knowing look. "That's just how Avery is. Don't worry. She kind of keeps to herself."

"I see." I pursed my lips, not liking how sad the little girl looked. Like she didn't have a friend in the world. All the other kids were laughing and joking—ignoring her completely, as if she weren't even in the room.

I wondered if I should leave her alone too—maybe that was what she wanted. But no . . . something in her face told me that wasn't it. There was a hint of longing in her eyes. As if she wanted to join in but couldn't bring herself to do it.

And so, as my friends settled the others into a

semicircle, leading them in a rousing rendition of "Let it Go," I headed over to her.

"Did you want to join them?" I asked, keeping my voice low.

She didn't look up. Just stared at the floor and shook her head.

"Yeah. I don't blame you," I told her in a confidential tone. "Between you and me, my friends aren't very good singers." I made a show of putting my hands over my ears and wrinkling my nose.

"They're okay," she said, in a voice barely louder than a whisper. "And the others like to sing."

"But you don't?"

"I do. I used to sing at my church all the time. It's just . . ." She shrugged and trailed off.

"You don't want to sing here," I concluded.

"I don't want to *be* here," she corrected. "I was supposed to be home by now. They promised I would be home in time for Easter."

"So you could sing with your church?"

She looked up, as if surprised. "Yes," she said solemnly.

I gave her a rueful look. "That stinks. I'm sorry."

She sighed. "Everyone's sorry. But no one can do anything about it. All these other kids? They're going home in a few weeks or whatever. And I'm going to be stuck here forever."

I watched as her eyes drifted over to the party again. My heart hurt at how sad she looked. Cinderella, who wouldn't allow herself to go to the ball. If only I had some real-life fairy godmother magic to help . . .

Wait a second . . .

A sudden idea struck me. Sure, I may not have had fairy godmother magic. But I still had a few tricks up my sleeve.

Literally, as Kalani would say.

I turned back to Avery. "Listen," I said, "I don't know if you'd be up for this, but I could actually use your help. You see, after the whole singing thing? I'm supposed to this magic show for everyone. And the thing is—I don't have a magician's assistant to help me. And we all know, you can't do a magic show without a magician's assistant."

She gave me a wary look. I rushed to continue before she could shoot me down. "I don't suppose you know anything about magic—"

"Actually, I do," she said shyly, surprising me with her answer.

"You do? Really?"

She nodded. "My brother does magic. He's really good. And he's shown me some of his tricks."

I grinned widely. "That's great!" I cried. "Then you can totally help me out."

I reached into my sack, pulled out my magic snow powder, and placed the bag in her hands. She took it from me and looked it over, cautious excitement lighting up her face.

"You really want me to be your assistant?" she asked.

"I *need* you to be," I corrected. "Otherwise my show is going to fail miserably." I paused, then added, "What do you say? Can you help a princess out?"

A small smile crossed her face. "I think I can do that."

I knew in my heart that when it came to magic tricks, I would probably never reach the Collin Prince level of awesome. But even I had to admit, this had been my best show yet. Especially with little Avery as my right-hand girl. Seriously, you'd never know by watching us that we hadn't been a team for years. She seemed to anticipate my every move—and it was like she knew almost all my tricks before I even announced them. In fact, she was so versed on some of them that I wondered if maybe she watched Collin Prince videos too.

The other kids ate up the show. And after we were finished, they all crowded around Avery to see her magic wand and ask her how she did the tricks. Her face was shining, alive, excited as she demonstrated, no longer the outsider of the group.

I grinned to myself. Mission accomplished. Cinderella had arrived at the ball.

Out of the corner of my eye I saw the nurse I had talked to earlier standing in the doorway, her eyes looking rather red. I slipped away from the party to go talk to her.

"Are you okay?" I asked.

She nodded, a lone tear slipping down her cheek. "Yes. I'm fine," she assured me. "It's just . . . I like seeing them like this. Especially Avery. Honestly, I don't think I've ever seen the girl crack a smile before tonight. She's such a serious child, carrying the weight of the world on her back. So to see her like this—laughing and playing with the other kids . . ." She shook her head, gazing at me with grateful eyes. "Thank you," she said. "Seriously, the memories of this night are going to go a long way in keeping their spirits up. Exactly what they'll need to get through the tough days ahead."

I looked back at Avery, the tears welling in my eyes. I didn't bother to brush them away. "Can I come back?" I asked the nurse. "I mean, just to visit sometime?"

She nodded. "I'm sure Avery would love that. All of them would."

I smiled. "I would love it too."

33

"WELL, THAT WAS AMAZING," MADISON ANNOUNCED, WALK-
ing into my bedroom Sunday morning. Her house was
still under construction, so we'd chosen to rendezvous
here instead. The plan was for us to watch all the new
Collin Prince videos, as per tradition, then head down
to the thrift store later and sell back our dresses as we'd
talked about.

Except . . . now I wasn't so sure. I mean, yes, it'd be
nice to buy new, more practical clothes. Clothes that
actually fit in my closet. But then this whole thing we'd
started would all be over for good. There'd be no going
back. No more princess babysitting. Or princess hospital
visiting. The thought made me a little sad.

"It was," I agreed, looking down at my phone and scrolling through all the photos I'd taken over the course of the evening. My friends and me—fully princessed and pirated out—posing with the little kids. My heart squeezed at the happy looks on everyone's faces. Not just the patients, either. My friends' smiles were just as big as the kids'.

Which didn't surprise me. After all, it had been an epic night.

I stopped at the last picture. Of little Avery and me doing our magic show. I felt my throat choke up a little as I looked down at Avery's shining face. A far more precious photo, in my opinion, than any snapshot of me and Collin Prince could ever be.

We had done well—and we had done good. That was all that mattered in the end.

"Maybe we shouldn't sell the dresses," Kalani broke in suddenly, as if reading my mind. When we all turned to look at her, she shrugged. "I don't know. What's the harm in keeping them? For . . . special occasions or whatever. There's got to be other hospitals who need princesses, right? Maybe that could become our new thing. In the summer, anyway, so it doesn't interfere with school."

Sarah nodded slowly. "That'd be cool," she agreed. "I had so much fun last night. I kind of forgot we weren't making any money."

"It was way better than any amount of money," I declared. "We got to use our princess powers for good. There's nothing better than that."

"Well, maybe one thing . . ." We looked up, surprised to see my stepmother walk into the room. She had a big smile on her face. "Oh good," she said. "You're all here."

I cocked my head in question. "What's up?" I asked.

"I just wanted to come by and thank you girls for doing such an amazing job last night," she said. "The hospital e-mailed the St. Francis Group this morning to tell me how great you were—and how you made the night so magical for those little kids. Evidently, they haven't stopped talking about you since."

I grinned, my heart warming at her words. "It was fun," I assured her. "We were happy to do it."

"Anytime they want us to come back, we're there," added Sarah. She looked at us questioningly. "Right?"

We all nodded. "Right," Kalani declared, smiling happily. "Anytime they need us."

My stepmother raised an eyebrow. "Even if they can't pay you?"

"We wouldn't let them pay us," Madison declared. "Even if they tried."

"Well then," my stepmother said, nodding thoughtfully, "I will definitely let them know that." She smiled. "I'm proud of you girls. You did a good thing." She paused, then added mysteriously, "And I think there's someone else who wants to thank you as well."

"What?" We looked at her, confused. What was she talking about?

We watched as she stepped over to the bed, grabbed the iPad and clicked it on, then propped it up on a pillow. A moment later, to our surprise, Collin Prince's YouTube channel popped up on the screen.

"He has a new video," she said. Then she laughed at our puzzled faces. "That's what you girls do, right? You meet up to watch his new videos?"

"Yeah, but . . ." I was so confused. Since when did Nancy actually care about Collin Prince?

She didn't reply. Just reached over and hit play. A moment later, Collin Prince sprang to life on the screen, and we all sighed in unison at the glimpse of his handsome face. Even though we'd probably never get the chance to meet him in real life, at least we'd never lose him online. That was something. In fact, it was a lot.

I tuned back in to the video.

"Hey, party people!" Collin was saying brightly, as was his usual opener. "How's it hanging in real-life land?" He paused, waggling his eyebrows, and the video cut to the opening music sequence. We grinned at one another, feeling that familiar buzz of anticipation we got in our stomachs every time he did a new video.

But this time, when the video cut back to him, to our surprise his smile had faded and his face had taken on an ultraserious look. I glanced at my friends, puzzled. They shrugged in response.

I turned back to the screen.

"Listen up, guys. I know I joke around a lot on this channel," Collin was saying. "But today I want to talk about something serious." He paused, clearing his throat. "If you don't want to hear it, feel free to click on one of my other videos below. May I suggest the one where I stick a pixie stick up my nose? That one's classic, right?"

Then he got serious again. "Most of you don't know this. It's not something I talk about a lot on the show. But

I have a little sister who's very sick. She's suffering from leukemia and has been in the hospital for most of the last year." He sighed. "It's been really hard on her. On all of us, actually—but mostly her. And for the last year, I haven't seen my baby sister smile. Not even once." He paused, then looked directly into the camera. "Until now."

I stared at the video, my heart suddenly pounding in my chest. I glanced up at my stepmother, but she only motioned for me to keep watching. As I turned back to the screen, the webcast cut from Collin's face to a low-light, grainy video.

A video of me. And my friends. Dancing in the hospital playroom.

I watched, stunned, as the video played. Of the four of us, singing and dancing and, looking like crazy fools. Of Avery assisting me with my magic show, grinning from ear to ear. Then the video cut again, switching to a still photo of me and Avery. The very same photo I'd just been looking at on my own phone—now full screen on Collin Prince's YouTube channel.

Oh. My. Gosh. OH MY GOSH.

"Hold on a second!" Madison cried, reaching out to stop the video. "Are you trying to tell me that little girl

Avery is Collin Prince's sister?" She turned to me accusingly. "Did you know about this?"

"I . . . had no idea!" I was barely able to speak I was so shocked. I looked back to my stepmother. "Did you?"

She gave me a conspiratorial smile. "I might have been made aware," she confessed.

"Why didn't you tell us?"

She shrugged. "I wasn't a hundred percent sure she'd be there," she said. "And also, I didn't want that to be the reason you decided to do the event. I wanted you to do it because you wanted to. Not because you'd get some reward."

I nodded slowly. That made sense. But still!

"That said," she added with a small smile, "I might have been the one to e-mail him the video he's playing on his channel right now . . . along with a little letter, letting him know you guys were fans." She smirked. "Not to mention that he still owed me that last math assignment he never turned in. Not that I'm holding my breath on that one."

Sarah reached out and unpaused the video. The picture of Avery and me faded away, and the screen went back to Collin.

"Those princesses and pirates last night," he said, his voice cracking, "they made my sister smile. For the first time since . . ." He trailed off, as if he was unable to speak. Then he swallowed hard. "My baby sister." He shook his head, holding up his hand. "Hang on a second."

The video jumped. He must have stopped the recording and started it again. When he came back to the screen, he wasn't crying anymore. (Though meanwhile the rest of us were bawling like babies.)

"Girls," he said. "I was told you watch my show. And if you're watching now, listen up. As you probably know, in June I'll be in Texas, appearing at the Comicpalooza convention." He smiled. "And I would be honored to have you there as my special guests. I can provide tickets and transportation for you and your parents, along with two nights' stay in a nearby hotel. You'll also get VIP passes to come see my magic show. And after the show I'd like to invite you backstage so I can personally thank you for what you did for my sister." He gave a big smile. "I know it's not much. But I hope you will come."

And with that the video stopped. We stared at the blank screen for a moment, in complete silence, as if all of us were trying to digest what we'd just heard. Then

Kalani let out a small scream. We all joined her, leaping up onto my bed and jumping up and down, screeching and cheering at the top of our lungs.

My stepmother covered her ears with her hands and laughed. "Um, I take it you want to accept his offer?" she asked, her eyes sparkling.

I shook my head. I couldn't believe it. Evil step-mother? Try fairy godmother!

And just like that, we were going to Comicpalooza after all.

34

A FEW DAYS LATER i FOUND MYSELF WALKiNG iNTO BRODY'S house. Following him through the hall toward his father's office. Now that I was back in business to go to Comicpalooza, I needed to finalize my writing project. I still wanted to enter the short story contest, after all, and I needed any help I could get.

"Hailey, this is my dad. Dad, this is Hailey."

I stepped hesitantly into the room. Brody's father rose from his seat, giving me a smile and reaching out to shake my hand, as if I were an actual adult. I looked around the room, a little in awe to see the tall bookcases filled with copies of his books. In addition to the American ones, it appeared there were translated copies from around the world. I tried to imagine my own office someday, with translated books. How cool would that be?

"Nice to meet you, Hailey. Brody has told me a lot about you."

I felt my face heat at this. "Um, he's told me a lot about you, too," I blurted.

"Why don't you have a seat? And Brody? Can you go get us some lemonade?"

"Sure." Brody dashed out of the room. Once he was gone, his father turned to me.

"So," he said. "I read your story. Both of them, actually."

My heart beat wildly in my chest. "I am so sorry about that!" I cried. "The other one is just some silly thing I write with my friend. I didn't mean to send it to you. I got the addresses mixed up and—"

"It was great."

"Wait, what? You mean the other story."

"That was a good story, too," he said. "I could tell you spent a long time on it. Really trying to make it good."

"Um, yes. I—"

"But the one you wrote with your friend? *That* one was great."

I stared at him, uncomprehending. "I don't

understand. That's just . . . fan fiction. It's not anything important or even—"

He held up a hand. "It's fun. It's compulsively readable. I couldn't put it down."

I sank back in my chair, utterly confused at this point. "But . . ."

"Look, when I read your short story, I could tell that you wanted very badly for people to love it," he said. "But when I read your Collin Prince story? I could tell how much *you* loved it. There was this energy, this enthusiasm. The words seemed to just jump off the page." He shrugged. "Honestly, I think that's the one you ought to submit to the contest."

"Are you serious?" I couldn't believe it. After all the agonizing I'd done over the serious story, he was suggesting I submit the fan fiction? Sarah was going to completely flip out! "Can I even do that?"

"You'd have to do a little work on it," he admitted. "Change the names to protect the innocent and all that. But in the end, this story isn't actually about Collin Prince, the YouTube star, is it? It's about a fictional character you created that you then named Collin Prince."

"I suppose that's true," I mused. After all, while

Collin had definitely been my inspiration from the start, the character in the actual story had long ago taken on a life of his own. I doubted Collin himself would recognize it if I changed the name. "So you really think I should submit this story to Comicpalooza?"

"Well, I have a few ideas and notes if you're open to suggestion," Brody's father said. "Things that could make the story stronger. But yes, between the two stories, this is the one you should submit. It's extremely engaging. And your true voice really comes out in the dialogue. That's what editors are looking for. What people want to read."

I nodded slowly, allowing his words to sink in. He was right, I realized. I loved the Collin Prince—or whatever it was we would call the character now—story. Way more than the story I wrote for the contest. So why did I think other people wouldn't like it too?

"Thank you," I said, rising to my feet. "You've given me a lot to think about."

He handed me a stack of computer printouts, which he had marked up in red pen. "I worked on both stories," he told me. "I didn't want to force your hand. At the end of the day, you're the author, Hailey. It's up to you to decide which you'd like to submit."

I took them from him, sucking in a breath. "Thank you," I said, turning to leave, my knees still feeling a little wobbly as I headed toward the door. "I really appreciate this. More than you know."

"You're a good writer, Hailey Smith," Brody's father called out to me as I left. "Keep it up and I'm sure I'll be seeing your books on store shelves someday."

I grinned. Now *that* would be a dream come true.

EPILOGUE

AND SO WE PRINCESSES WENT TO THE BALL. NOT IN THE COSTUMES we had originally planned, but in our princess and pirate best. After all, that was what got us here in the first place. And we figured there was some kind of magic in that.

What can I say about Comicpalooza? It was massive. A little scary, too. Thousands of people wandering around in costume, taking in the sights. Tables filled with cool sci-fi/fantasy toys. There was tons of game-related stuff to buy, and I picked up a Fields of Fantasy T-shirt for Brody that I thought he would like. He was here somewhere too. With his dad. But we hadn't seen him yet. Not surprising. This place was huge!

Oh, and I know you want to hear about meeting

Collin Prince. It was pretty epic, to say the least. His show was amazing, and going backstage afterward made us feel like superstars. He hugged each of us and thanked us in turn and gave us each little homemade cardboard hearts his sister had made us from the hospital. It felt really good. And Kalani swore she would literally never wash her hands again. (A vow that lasted about ten minutes after a huge Klingon managed to bump into her and spill his Diet Coke. Ah well.)

But the real highlight of the convention? Having all my best friends with me on the final night as we sat in the audience of the writers' track's closing session where they would announce the winners of the young writers' competition.

"I'm probably not going to win, you know," I reminded them for the thousandth time as the crowd ushered in.

"Please," Madison scoffed. "You're a great writer, Hailey. If they don't pick you, they have a serious problem."

"Just don't forget us little people when you're rich and famous," Kalani added with a grin.

I snorted. Before I could reply, my eyes caught sight of a man dressed in a suit and tie walking up to the podium. My pulse kicked up its pace as I watched him attempt to get the microphone into position before starting to speak.

"That's my dad's editor."

I looked up to see that Brody had slipped into the row next to us. Sarah scooted over so he could sit next to me.

"Good luck," he whispered. "I hope you win."

I looked around at my friends. Then I looked at Brody and smiled. "Trust me," I said. "No matter what happens with the contest, I already have."

The man at the podium cleared his throat. "Thank you all for coming this afternoon. I hope you have had a great show so far. And I appreciate everyone who participated in our little writers' track. We love having you as part of our family each year." He smiled. "And now, because I know you all have parties to go to, I will get to the point. The winners of the annual Comicpalooza writing competitions." He looked down at his notes. "First up, the adult sci-fi fantasy category . . ."

He rambled off a name. People cheered. The winner got up and made a little speech. I tried to pay attention, but all the while my heart was beating furiously in my chest. The winner sat down and the editor came back, reading off the name of another adult category, and I realized I might die of anticipation before he got to the young writer award.

"I can't stand it," I whispered to Brody. He reached out and squeezed my hand with his own, then left it there, covering mine. Okay, now *that* was a suitable distraction. If it didn't cause me to pass out altogether.

After what seemed an eternity, Brody's dad's editor got to the last category. "The winner of the young writers' competition this year . . ." He grabbed the envelope and made a grand gesture of opening it as slowly as possible. I could barely breathe. Sarah and Madison and Kalani all reached over and gave me comforting squeezes.

This was it. This was the moment I'd been waiting for. Or not waiting for. Oh man.

"Well, well. It seems we actually have two winners this year," the man said, looking surprised. "A coauthor team." He smiled. "Guess that means we'll be sending two young authors to camp this summer!"

He gave a dramatic pause. It was all I could do not to puke on everyone in the audience. Finally he looked up.

"The winning story is . . . 'The Prince's Adventure,' authored by Hailey Smith and Sarah Farmington."

"Wait, what?" Sarah cried loudly, causing the entire audience to burst out laughing. She turned to me, confusion on her face. "I don't understand."

"Oh. Didn't I mention?" I asked innocently, my heart soaring in my chest. "I decided to submit *our* story to the contest instead. It was way better than the other one."

"Oh my gosh. Oh my gosh!" she cried, looking as if she was going to pass out. "You did not! You so did not!"

I grinned. "I so did too. Now come on. Everyone's waiting for us to get up there." I grabbed her arm and led her to the stage. She staggered after me, still looking dazed. When we got to the podium, she put her hand over the mic and turned to me.

"I hope you at least wrote a speech," she whispered. "'Cause I was so not planning on this."

I shook my head. "No speech," I told her. "But I'm sure we'll think of something. After all, we're pretty good at putting on a show."

ACKNOWLEDGMENTS

FIRST OFF, A SPECIAL THANK-YOU TO MY AWESOME EDITOR, Alyson Heller, and the entire team at Aladdin for believing in me and helping me take this book from imagination to bookstore shelf—and, most important, into the hands of readers. I couldn't do it without your support!

And to agent extraordinaire Mandy Hubbard at Emerald City Literary. This was our first book together, but definitely not our last! Your enthusiasm and passion make this sometimes tough job not only bearable, but actually fun!

To Jill and Greg Murphy, my very first babysitting charges way back in the day. You were definitely better behaved than any of the kids in this book! And you've grown up to be amazing adults, too. Love to you and your family.

To my husband, Jacob, who is always understanding when I'm on deadline. (And hates when people compare dad parenting to "babysitting.") And to Avalon, my darling girl—you were a major inspiration for this book. I'm only sorry your glow stick "adventure" didn't make the final cut!

To all the awesome librarians out there—both here in Texas and all over the country. You continually blow me away with your passion and enthusiasm and love for your kids. They are so lucky to have you, and I know their lives will be better for it. Keep that love of reading alive!

And to all you real-life princesses, pirates, babysitters, future authors, YouTube stars, and all the rest—keep following your dreams, wherever they may take you. And don't be afraid to fail sometimes. It only makes success that much sweeter in the end.

Don't miss another great read
from Mari Mancusi

"Hi there! I'm here to drop off Alexis Miller?"

I hugged my jacket closer to my chest as Mom slid down the rental-car window and addressed the man sitting in the guard shack outside Mountain Academy's wrought-iron front gate. It was only November, but the temperature had dropped, and the wind swirled through the car, stinging my still-sunburned nose. I breathed in, smelling hints of snow on the horizon. Most people didn't believe you could smell snow, but you could. There was this sweetness to the air just before the first flakes started to fall. The forecasters had predicted at least twelve to fifteen inches tonight, and Mom had decided to cut her trip short in order to get back to eighty-degree temperatures and sunshine. After having been married to my dad for twelve frost-bitten years, she'd say, she'd had enough of the white stuff to last a lifetime.

The gates creaked open and the guard waved Mom through, allowing us access to the long, windy road flanked by large oak trees that led to the main campus. We'd missed foliage season by a couple weeks, and the trees' once-colorful leaves had faded and fallen—now blanketing the road in corpses of beige. As the bright morning sun filtered through bare branches, peering curiously into the car, I slouched in my seat and slid on my sunglasses, missing the vibrant palm trees in Mom's backyard already.

Mountain Academy for Skiers and Snowboarders used to be a traditional New England boarding school— offering elite educations to children whose parents summered at Cape Cod and wintered in Saint Barts. And for a time it seemed that it would stay that way forever, mass-producing future lawyers and doctors and politicians from here to eternity and beyond.

But then, in 1969, the stuffy founder of this stuffy institution was found dead—facedown in a plate of stuffing. It was Thanksgiving. (I couldn't make this stuff up.) And the school ended up being passed down to his hippie-dippie fool of a grandson, Irving "Call me Moonbeam" Vandermarkson, who had somehow, over the years, managed to avoid becoming lawyer, doctor, or politician, even after graduating (barely) from his grandfather's prestigious school. In fact, Irving had somehow managed to avoid choosing a career at all. Until this one was dumped in his lap.

But Moonbeam wasn't interested in running a boring old boarding school like his grandfather. After all, he argued, there were plenty of other places to go if you wanted to suit up in a blazer and tie and pad your college application with Harvard-friendly extracurriculars. Moonbeam wanted to run a school where kids could learn something more spectacular than fractions and fiction and filling in the blanks.

Like skiing, for example. Moonbeam's favorite pastime.

So he quickly ejected the school's then-current crop

of future leaders of America and replaced them with a ragtag team of young but promising skiers, remodeling the place after one of those famous Russian sports schools founded in the 1930s. As you can imagine, the board of trustees was horrified! How embarrassing! The school's reputation would never recover after these scruffy juvenile delinquents with funny boots and sticks strapped to their feet began parading down its halls.

But, go figure, it turned out Irving Vandermarkson—dirty hippie and ski bum extraordinaire—was actually onto something. In fact, his disgraceful little ski boarding school became a raging success. Today, more than one hundred Mountain Academy graduates have earned a spot on a national team—with fifty-four of them competing in the Winter Olympics and thirty-nine becoming medal winners. The school went from being a total joke to *the* place to enroll if you were serious about your winter-sports career.

And I had always been serious. Until now.

"Do I *really* have to do this?" I asked for the umpteenth time since we'd gotten off the plane in New Hampshire. "I mean, why can't I stay in Florida with you this winter?" Hanging out with my friends on the beach, tanning and talking and flirting with cute lifeguards sounded so much better than freezing my butt off up here while trying to chase my dream for a second time.

Mom offered me a rueful smile. "I wish you could," she said, reaching over to pat me on the knee, while keeping an eye on the windy road, already slick with black ice. "More than anything. But I don't make the rules."

When my parents split up three years ago and my mom moved out of state, the court awarded my dad custody from September to May so I could continue attending Mountain Academy. This year, however, Mom had gotten special permission for me to stay down in the Sunshine State until I finished my physical therapy. But now the doctors had given me a clean bill of health, leaving me no other choice but to trek back to the frozen tundra for the remainder of the winter.

I'd tried to argue that I'd rather walk over hot coals in bare feet while listening to Justin Bieber songs on an endless loop than return to this place. While Mom certainly sympathized, there was nothing she could do.

"Here we are," she announced unnecessarily, forcing perkiness as she pulled the rental car up to the front entrance of the school. Like most fancy New England boarding schools, Mountain Academy boasted a redbrick facade, complete with the requisite Ivy League ivy withering on the walls. I used to think it looked pretty cool. Like an old Victorian mansion from one of my mother's beloved Jane Austen books. Now it resembled a prison.

I dragged myself out of the car, my legs feeling like lead, and walked around to retrieve my suitcase from the trunk. Most of my stuff was already here, stored at my dad's place, a little staff cabin a few yards from the boys' dorm. I used to live there with him, but last year, after much begging and pleading, he'd allowed me to move into the girls' dorm like everyone else. Which, at the time, had been a dream come true. Now, however, the idea of facing all the curious stares and pitying looks from the student body—not to mention the smug smile of my archnemesis, Olivia, herself—made me wish I could hide out in his cabin for the entire winter.

As I yanked the suitcase from the trunk and started lugging it toward the school, Mom scurried after me. "You sure you don't need help with that?" she asked, her eyes falling worriedly to the bag in question. Something she would have never asked me, I realized, before my accident.

"I'm fine," I muttered.

"Okay, okay," she agreed quickly. Too quickly—as if she'd realized what she'd implied and felt bad about it. She grabbed me by my shoulders and pulled me into a big hug.

"I'll miss you, baby," she whispered in my ear.

"I'll miss you too, Mom."

"You're going to be fine. Really. It won't be as bad as you think."

I squirmed away.

"I'm serious, Lexi. . . ." Her voice drifted off, and I could tell she was searching for something positive, and, of course, completely cliché to say in a vain attempt to make me feel better. Like how I should get right back on that horse. Or time heals all wounds. Or I should turn lemons into lemonade. Or maybe the most ridiculous one of all: *It doesn't matter if you win or lose; it's how you play the game.*

Yeah right. Tell that to the Olympic committee.

"It's okay, Mom." I tried to reassure her. "I'll be fine. Promise." I gave her my biggest, best fake smile. The one I'd been using all year long to satisfy concerned aunts and uncles and doctors and friends. The one that said, *I'm fine.* Even though I wasn't.

Mom met my eyes, as if not fooled for a second. Then

she sighed and planted a kiss on my nose like she used to do when I was little. "I know you will. You're my strong girl," she whispered, giving my shoulders a comforting squeeze. "My little warrior princess."

She started back to the car, then stopped. I watched her turn back slowly, her face a mess of mixed emotions. "Just . . . ," she started, then trailed off.

I furrowed my brow, wondering what she wanted to say. "Just what, Mom?" Was she finally going to tell me? Admit what I'd overheard the doctor say when he thought I wasn't listening? *She'll be able to snowboard again,* he'd told her. *But she may never be what she was before the accident.*

Which, in doctor speak, roughly translated to: *You know those silly little Olympic dreams? Yeah, not going to happen. Not in this lifetime anyway.*

Mom was silent, and I could practically see her warring thoughts battling one another inside her head. Then, at last, she sighed. "Just don't let him push you," she said in a quiet voice. "Trust your instincts. Go at your own pace. You have nothing to prove to anyone. Even if . . ." She trailed off again, and I knew she didn't want to say out loud what we both knew could be true.

"You're special," she amended. "No matter what. Never forget that."

Oh great. I could feel the lump rise to my throat. The tears well up in my eyes. I'd promised myself I wouldn't cry. Not here. Not where someone could see. So I swallowed down the lump and swiped away the tears, forcing myself to nod my head.

"I've got to go," I mumbled, grabbing my suitcase and turning to head toward the dorm. I could feel Mom's eyes on my back, watching as I stumbled under the main archway leading into campus, unable to help but catch the familiar school quote above me, etched in stone and echoed by teachers and coaches all over school.

What would you attempt to do, it asked, *if you knew you could not fail?*

I used to love that quote. I used to say it all the time. Wrote it in notebooks, stickered it to my board. The same board that had cracked in two that fateful December day when I learned the truth.

That I could indeed fail. And that failure really hurt.